Great Britain Folklore Society

The Folklore Record

Vol III Part I

Great Britain Folklore Society

The Folklore Record
Vol III Part I

ISBN/EAN: 9783744781824

Printed in Europe, USA, Canada, Australia, Japan

Cover: Foto ©Andreas Hilbeck / pixelio.de

More available books at **www.hansebooks.com**

The Folk-Lore Society,

FOR COLLECTING AND PRINTING

RELICS OF POPULAR ANTIQUITIES, &c.

ESTABLISHED IN

THE YEAR MDCCCLXXVIII.

Alter et Idem.

4 5 6 9 6
26 / 6 / 99

PUBLICATIONS
OF
THE FOLK-LORE SOCIETY.

V.

THE

FOLK-LORE RECORD,

VOL III. PART I.

LONDON:
PRINTED FOR THE FOLK-LORE SOCIETY,
BY MESSRS. NICHOLS & SONS,
25, PARLIAMENT STREET, WESTMINSTER, S.W.

1880.

CATSKIN;

THE ENGLISH AND IRISH PEAU D'ÂNE.

[Read at the first Evening Meeting of the Society, December 9th, 1879.]

GOLDSMITH, in a well-known passage of his *Vicar of Wakefield*, says that Sir William Thornhill, when he masqueraded in the Vicar's family under the name of Mr. Burchell, told the children among other things * the "Adventures of Catskin."

Here is a plain reference to a folk-tale, either of Goldsmith's own country or of his adopted country, or of both these countries. But, though the tale to deserve such a public recognition as the novelist has thus given it must have been necessarily then familiar to all sections of society, yet for more than a generation nothing has been known of its purport or contents in this country. It has indeed attained the honour of being a *crux* both in England and Germany. Though many distinguished folk-lorists of both these countries have zealously searched after it, not one of them has succeeded in discovering even a vestige of the lost story.

This want of success on the part of so many able antiquaries is the more remarkable as the story itself has never been a mystery in the land to which the author of the Vicar of Wakefield belonged. There it has been always known to all the wandering or sedentary *scealuidhes* —the Homers and Mudies of the peasantry—and their national frank-heartedness has never kept it a secret from any class.

---

* Book vi. The other stories named are *The Buck of Beverland, Patient Grizzell,* and *Fair Rosamond's Bower*, all English.

But if English antiquaries have found themselves at fault in regard to Irish Folk-Lore they have equally failed to hit off what should at least have afforded them a warmer scent ; they have never even suspected that England once possessed an original and native version of the same myth, and yet the one fact is quite as unquestionable as the other. The two folk-tales are still in existence, and I shall have no difficulty in removing the cloud which has accidentally enveloped them.

This I will do by laying the narratives textually before you. I will give the *pas* to the Irish tale, because it has much beauty which the other cannot boast, and it is also otherwise in better form and preservation. It was taken down some few years ago from the lips of a native *scealuidhe* by the late Mr. Patrick Kennedy, who had previously known it well as a boy in his native county of Wexford. In 1870 he published it with other tales, *ejusdem musae*, in a volume to which he gave the name of " Fireside Stories of Ireland." Mr. Kennedy is now dead, and praise is lost upon him. But I cannot refrain from saying that this charming volume, though coming after so many precious contributions to Folk-Lore in France, in Italy, and in Germany, contains old-world fictions which no other collection has surpassed in beauty or interest.

Out of respect for the law of copyright I have condensed the Irish tale in the following manner.

There was once a queen that was left a widow with a daughter, who was as good and handsome as any girl could be. The mother married again, and died soon after. At the end of the year the widower proposed to his daughter-in-law to marry her. In her distress, when the evening comes, she goes into the paddock where her filly was. The latter turns out to be a fairy, and advises her what to do. She is to consent to the marriage if her father-in-law will give her a dress of silk and silver thread that will fit into a walnut-shell. The princess does as she is bid, and half a year after the dress is ready. By the advice of the filly the princess insists on another dress —one of silk and gold thread that also will fit into a walnut-shell. After a greater delay this also is got for her, but before giving her final consent she tells her father-in-law she must have a dress of silk thread as thick as it can be with diamonds and pearls no larger than the head of a minnikin pin. The dress came home at last, and on the same evening the princess found on her bed another made of cat-skins, and this she put on, having first made her face and hands brown with a wash to disguise herself. She then put her three walnut-shells into her pocket, and stole out into the stable, where she found the filly bridled and saddled. Away they went, and when the light first appeared in the sky they were a hundred miles away. They stopped at the edge of a wood, and the princess got down and rested herself at the foot of a tree and slept soundly. She was awakened by the baying of hounds, and would have been torn in pieces by them if the young king of the country, whose hounds they were, had not whipped them off. The young king, who sees her beauty through her catskins, takes her to the hall-door of his house and hands her over to his housekeeper, telling her to find her some employment. But the housekeeper gave her nothing better to do than to help the scullery-maid, and at night she had to sleep under the stairs. The next day the prince ordered that the new servant should bring him up a basin and towel to wash himself before dinner. She took up the things, and the prince delayed her ever so long with remarks and questions, striving to get out of her who she was, for he guessed her to be a lady. Next night the prince was at a ball about three miles off, and the princess got leave from the housekeeper to go early to bed. But she could not get herself to lie down; she stepped out into the lawn, and there saw the filly under a tree. The latter tells her to take out one of the walnut-shells. She does so, and on opening it finds the silk and silver dress. She puts it over her head, and it fits beau-tifully. "Jump into the saddle," says the filly, and in a few minutes they were at the hall door of the castle where the ball was. There she sprang from her saddle, and walked in. Lights were in the hall and everywhere, and nothing could equal the glitter of the princess's robes. Says the Irish *scealuidhe* (storyteller), "it was like the curling of a stream in the sun." She made a great sensation, and the prince danced with her and fell in love with her. She bade him farewell, and he saw her to the hall door, where she mounted the filly, and they were away like a flash of lightning in the dark night. Next morning he sent for her to bring hot water and a towel for him to shave. She came. Whenever the prince got a peep at her face there were the beautiful eyes and nose and mouth of the lady in the glittering dress, but all as brown as a bit of bogwood. He asked her if she was of high birth, but she turned the discourse.

There was another great ball in a week's time, and the very same thing took place again. There was the princess, and the dress she had on was the silk and gold thread. The prince became more enamoured, and before leaving she promised to come to the next ball. When she and the filly came under the tree on the lawn she took the upper end of her dress in her fingers, and it came off like a glove, and she made her way in at the back door, and into her crib at the stair-foot. In the morning the prince sent for the girl in the catskins to bring up a needle and thread to sew a button on his shirt-sleeve. He watched her fingers and saw they were small and lovely; but when the button was sewed she slipped downstairs.

The third night came, and she shook the dress of silk and pearls and diamonds over her, and went to the ball. There in the course of the evening he asked her to marry him. She replied, " You will see me again, and if you know me when you meet me next we will part no more." When the prince afterwards held her hand as she was going away at the hall-door he slipped a dawny ring of gold on her finger without her feeling it. Next morning he sent for her, and told her he was going to be married. " I have asked you twice already," said he, " to be my queen ; I ask you now, the third time. You promised me you would have me if I knew you the next time we should meet. This is the next time. If I don't know you, I know my ring on your fourth finger." She asked his permission to leave the room. She went out and returned shortly with the brown stain off her face and hands, and her dazzling dress of silk and jewels on her. They did not put off their marriage.

There can be no question, after reading Mr. Kennedy's story, that it is the tale, or one of the tales, to which Goldsmith referred.

But as the *dramatis personæ* of his celebrated novel are English people, and the scene is laid in England, it might also be inferred that Goldsmith knew there was an English folk-tale recounting the same adventures of the same heroine; and when he made Mr. Burchell tell his story to his young English friends, together with other purely English stories (be it observed) (see note at p. 1), he meant it to be supposed that that gentleman followed an English and not an Irish version. If we take that to be Goldsmith's meaning, our supposition has certainly its foundation in fact, for there was then in actual existence an English version—one which Mr. Burchell as an Englishman and given to story-telling would, if he had been himself a reality, by necessity have adopted.

This English version also it will be my pleasure to lay before the present company, but before giving the tale textually I must shortly explain in what form and by what means it has come down to us.

Mr. Halliwell Phillipps, in his *Nursery Rhymes of England*, first published by him in 1841, inserted a poetical tale (No. 104) which he entitled "The Story of Catskin." * In its style and diction this poem is as pompous and vapid as the famous "Beggar's Petition," and it may therefore, in the form given by Mr. H. Phillipps, be assigned to about the same date—the middle of the last century. Mr. Phillipps himself took it down at some date previous to 1841 from a nurse aged 81.

Put into humble prose this English story will read as follows:—

"A grand country gentleman, who has had only daughters and no son born to him, declares to his wife in a fit of temper that if another daughter arrives she shall never stay in his house. Another daughter is born, and is immediately sent out of the house and afterwards to school, where she remains until she is fifteen. Finding the prohibition still in force at home, the poor girl determines to go into service. She rolls up her grand and gay dresses in a bundle, and hides them in a forest, and then puts on a catskin robe. She starts in this attire and

---

* *The Nursery Rhymes of England*, by J. O. Halliwell, Esq. second edition with additions, 1843; first edition in 1841. Upon this story Mr. W. H. Phillipps has the following observation: "As related by an old nurse, aged eighty-one. The story is of Oriental origin; but the song, as recited, was so very imperfect, that a few necessary additions and alterations have been made." From this modified remark we have a right to infer that neither the additions nor alterations have been material.

proceeds on her journey until she comes to a castle. The dowager lady of the castle is so struck with her great beauty when she prays for charity that she engages her as scullion.

In this castle Catskin leads a very sad life under the cook, who often takes a ladle and breaks her head with it.

Soon after her coming there is to be a great ball, and Catskin in her youthful spirits tells the cook that she should very much like to go to it. The cook insultingly replies that she would· cut a fine figure amongst the company in her catskin robe, and at the same time she cruelly dashes a basin of water in the face of the disguised young lady. Poor Catskin shakes her ears and goes to her hiding-place in the forest, and there washes away every stain from her face at a crystal waterfall. She also puts on a beautiful dress, one of those which she had brought away with her, and then hastens off to the ball. On her appearance there the ladies are struck dumb at her figure and face. Her young master falls in love with her beauty and grace, and dances with her the whole night. When the time for leaving comes he asks her where she lives, to which she evasively replies, "At the sign of the basin of water I dwell," and flies from the ball-room. When she gets back to the forest she puts on her catskin robe again, and slips into the house unseen by the cook, who little thinks where the scullion has been.

Next day the young lord tells his passion to his mother, and declares that he shall never be able to rest until he shall have found out this beautiful maid.

Another grand ball is accordingly to be given. Catskin expresses to the cook a similar wish to go to that as to the other, and she is again insulted by her as on the first occasion. The cook also in a rage takes up the ladle again, and again breaks Catskin's head with it. Off she goes notwithstanding, shaking her ears. She flies swiftly to the forest. There she washes off every bloodstain, puts on another of her dresses, more beautiful than the first, and hastens to the ball. The young lord, longing to see her again, is waiting for her at the door of the ball-room, and he dances with her all the night. He again asks her at parting where she lives. Her only answer is, "At the sign of the broken ladle I dwell." Then she flies to the forest, re-assumes her catskin robe, and slips into her own room unseen by the cook, who little thinks where her scullion has been.

Next day the young lord again declares to his mother that he shall never be happy until he finds the young lady who has charmed him so much. Accordingly another ball is appointed, Catskin repeats her old wish to the cook, and again her head is broken by the menial, but with the skimmer this time. Heartwhole, not-withstanding, and lively as ever, Catskin is off to the forest, where she washes away the bloodstains at the crystal waterfall, puts on the most beautiful of her dresses, and hastens away to the ball. There the young lord, who is waiting for her at the ballroom door, dances with her exclusively all night long; at parting he asks her where she lives. "At the sign of the Broken Skimmer I dwell," is her only answer. Then she flies to the forest, puts on again her catskin cloak (as it is now called), and slips into the house unseen by the cook, who little thinks where the young servant has been.

But my lord had seen her, for he followed her too fast. Hid in the green forest, he is a witness to the strange things that pass on this as on the other occasions.

Next day he takes to his bed, and sends for the doctor, to whom he confides his affection for Catskin, and declares that his heart will break without her. He also begs him to allow no one but Catskin to come into his room. The doctor intercedes with the proud lady mother, who yields to her son's wish, only because she fears he will die.

After thus obtaining his mother's consent the young lord gets well quickly, and is married to Catskin.

Before a twelvemonth is over Lady Catskin gives birth to a young lord. One day the child, having given an alms to a beggar's child, the grandmother, who is called a wicked old woman, observes, " Only see how the beggars' brats take to each other." Catskin, shocked at this taunt, prevails on her husband to join her in search of her father. The latter, who in the meanwhile has lost all his other cilldren, is easily found. My Lord leaves Catskin at the head inn of the town near where the father resides, and goes and breaks the matter to him. The repentant old gentleman is overjoyed at the news, and heartily welcomes his daughter and grandchild when they are brought to him.

It cannot be disputed, I think, that these two stories—the English and Irish—are identical in motive and plot. The minor differences which are visible between them are only such as spring up insensibly, according as the same stories are told by different people in different countries.

There must, therefore, have been the same origin to both, Ireland, I mean the Irish pale, receiving the story directly from England. What the remote origin of each of them was I will presently show. But, before doing so, I will state what is not the least interesting circumstance connected with this old tale.

A corresponding Folk-Tale is found diffused through every inter- vening country from the Himalayas to Ireland. It is told in France, in Italy, in Spain, in Germany, in Russia, in Lithuania, in Greece, and in Albania, as well as in England and Ireland. The Scottish Gael and the Lowlanders of North Britain equally also possess it.[*]

In France the story has been a favourite from all time under the slightly different title of " Peau d'âne," or Ass's skin, from the varia- tion in the disguise assumed by the heroine.[†]

As Peau d'âne may be taken almost as the representative story of this class of myths, owing to the position to which French literature elevates everything which it touches, and as it is not so well known in England as it ought to be, I will lay it before the present com- pany, abstracting it as briefly as possible.

" A certain king, having lost his wife, and mourned for her even more than other men do, suddenly determines, by way of relieving his sorrows, to marry his own daughter. The princess obtains a sus- pension of this odious purpose by requiring from him three beautiful dresses, which take a long time to prepare. These dresses are a robe

---

[*] See Deulin's *Contes de ma mère l'Oye*, under the head *Peau d'âne*, pp. 83- 126.

[†] For *Peau d'âne*, see Hetzel's edition (Paris) of *Les Contes de Perrault*, p. 43, *et seqq.*

of the colour of the sky (*de la couleur du temps*), a robe of the colour of the moon, and a third robe of the colour of the sun, the latter being embroidered with the rubies and diamonds of his crown. The three dresses being made and presented to her, the princess is check-mated, and accordingly asks for something even more valuable in its way. The king has an ass that produces gold coins in profusion every day of his life. This ass the princess asked might be sacrificed, in order that she might have his skin. This desire even was granted. The princess, thus defeated altogether, puts on the ass's skin, rubs her face over with soot, and runs away. She takes a situation with a farmer's wife, to tend the sheep and turkeys of the farm.

Whilst in this service, Peau d'âne occasionally washes her face at a fountain, and puts on one or other of her beautiful dresses in the little room that is allotted to her at the farmhouse. There the king's son accidentally saw her one day in all her splendour by looking through the keyhole, and is told, in answer to his inquiry, that the inhabitant of this little room is only a dirty-faced girl on the farm, who is, for obvious reasons, called Peau d'âne. The prince, overcome, falls sick and takes to his bed, and on being questioned by the queen his mother what can be done for him, he says, I wish Peau d'âne to make me a cake. She makes him the cake, and drops a ring into it. The prince eats it so eagerly that the ring nearly chokes him. Love gets a greater hold over him and he becomes worse, and at last he declares to the queen that he will marry only the young person whose finger the ring will fit. The king and queen consent, and proclamation is made to all to come to the palace and try on the ring, and that she whom it will fit shall be married to the prince. Crowds of women of all ranks try it, but in vain. " Have you sent for Peau d'âne," says the prince, "who made me the cake?" She is sent for and tries on the ring, which of course fits. Her ass's skin falls off, and she appears in her silver dress, and is found out to be a princess, and is straightway married to the prince.

Italy has several versions of the same tale. Three of the most striking I will give. They are called " La Zuccaccia " (Ugly Gourd), " L'orso " (the Bear), and " Il trottolin di legno " (Wooden Top).

The first-named, which in its commencement closely resembles the French story, is to the following effect:[*]—

The princess, when she finds that the king, her father, is in earnest, runs away from him with the assistance of her nurse. She previously puts on a cambric dress, stitched all over with pieces of dried gourd. She takes away with her three beautiful dresses that her father has given, upon similar conditions as in the French story. Zuccaccia, as she is called from the dress, is after her flight taken into the service of a king, into whose country she and the nurse have penetrated, as a stable-help and scullion.

One day the king's son goes into the kitchen and tells her that it is his custom to give three balls in the year, and invites her to the first, and, as he speaks, he raps her knees with the fire-shovel. She puts on one of her three dresses—a silk dress, colour of the air, and bestrewn with the stars of the heavens, and goes to the ball. The prince dances with her all night long. He asks her her name, who she is, where she has come from, but all he can get from her is, "I am from Rap shovel upon the knees." The prince gives her a gold hairpin, which he then and there puts into her tresses. She gets away unnoticed. A second ball is to be given, and the prince goes into the kitchen to tell her of it. He invites her to this also, and whilst he is speaking he taps her over the shoulders with his riding-whip. She goes to this ball also, but more splendidly dressed than ever, for she has on a silk dress the colour of sea-water, with gold fishes swimming in it. She dances with the prince, who asks her the same question as before. Her only answer is that her country is called "Rap whip upon the shoulders." The prince gives her a ring with his name engraved on the stone. She gets away unobserved. The next morning the prince goes into the kitchen to tell her all that has happened, and while talking raps her over the feet with the tongs. She goes to the third ball, wearing a dress interwoven with little bells and chains of gold. To the prince's old question where she comes from, her answer is, "From Rap tongs upon the feet." The prince gives her a

[*] It is No. 57 of Comparetti's invaluable collection of *Novellino popolari Italiane*.

medallion portrait of himself. She gets away as before, and the prince
falls ill with love of her. He tells the queen, his mother, that he has
a wish for some soup, and that Ugly Gourd (Zuccaccia) must make it.
She makes it, and puts the gold pin into it; after taking it he asks for
more, and the ring and the portrait are successively served up to him.
Then he gets up, goes down, and finds out the whole secret, and is
married to Ugly Gourd. Her father is invited to the feast, and
recognises his daughter.

The second of these stories (the Bear) is to the following effect:*—

A king who had an only daughter was so fond of her that he kept her
always in doors. She complained about it to her nurse, who was a witch,
and the latter told her to ask her father to give her a wooden grotto
and a bear-skin. When the young girl had obtained them she went
to the witch, who so enchanted the grotto that it would move at a
gesture from the princess. The princess put on the bear-skin, and
set off with the grotto, until she came to a wood where she hid herself in a thicket. A prince is hunting there, and has to call off his
dogs, who attack the princess. The prince invites her home, and she
and the grotto set off together to the palace, where she becomes a
servant. One day the prince tells his mother that he shall go to a
ball. The bear, who is under the table, says, " Let me go too," but he
cuffs her and drives her away. The queen-mother, however, gives her
permission, and she runs away to the grotto, and with a magic wand
that the witch had given her calls up a beautiful dress with a pattern
like the moon on it, and a carriage and pair. She enters the carriage
and goes to the ball, where the prince falls in love with her and dances
several times with her. As soon as the ball is over she flies. There
is a second ball, and both go there, the princess more beautiful still
from the dress like the sun which she had put on. She dances with
the prince and flies as before. There is a third ball, and both are
there again, she in a dress strewn with gems,—never had been seen
anything more beautiful and more rich. The prince dances with her
and slips a ring on her finger. When the time for leaving comes she

* *Fiabe Mantovane, raccolte da Isaia Visentini*, vol. vii. of *Canti'e racconti
del popolo Italiano*, p. 177, *et seqq.* No. 38.

flies as before. The prince comes home, and being dead tired (*stracco morto*) asks for soup. The bear brings it to him, but first drops the ring into the platter. The prince finds it, and seizing the bear makes her take off the skin, and she appears still in her ball-dress of gems which she had not taken off. After that they are married.

The other Italian tale (the Wooden Top) is to this effect :*—

A widower, who had promised his wife that he would marry the woman only whose finger her ring would fit, determines to marry his own daughter, because it has accidentally turned out that the ring fits her.

By the advice of an old woman, the daughter asks her father for three dresses, one with little gold bells, one with gold fishes, and one with stars upon it. When these dresses are given, she asks her father for a wooden top, and, having got it, gets inside of it and flies. The old woman previously gives her a magic wand for use when the necessity shall arise. A marquis who meets the top rolling along takes it into his service, and she thereupon comes out of it. One evening the marquis is going to a ball; she asks him to take her there. He refuses, and she raps his knees with the tongs. On his leaving home she obtains through the wand a carriage and pair, and, having put on her the first of the three dresses, goes to the ball. There she makes a general sensation, and the marquis falls in love with her. He asks her where she comes from. " From Rap tongs," says she. The next day, as the marquis intends going again to the ball, she repeats her request, and is again refused, whereupon she knocks his knees with a broom. She now obtains, through the wand, a carriage and four, and, having put on her second dress, goes off again to the ball. The marquis becomes still more enamoured, and asks her again where she has come from. " From Knock broom," says she. The third day, as she finds that the marquis is again going to the ball, she again asks him to take her, and he again refuses, whereupon she takes up a fire-shovel and raps him over the knee with it. She now obtains from the wand

* Gubernatis's *Novelline di Santo Spirito, di Calcinaia*, No. 3.

a carriage and six and goes a third time to the ball, after putting on her last dress. There she enchants the marquis entirely. He asks her for a third time where she comes from. "From Rap fire-shovel," says she. She then gets into her carriage and drives off. The next day she pretends to be ill, and shuts herself up in her room, and through the power of the wand makes herself marvellously beautiful. She seats herself on a sofa and spreads her three dresses around her. The marquis searches for her over the house, and finds her at last in her room, and then marries her.

Germany also has a most interesting version.

It is called Allerleirauh (or all sorts of rough), and is to the following purport :*—

A king insists upon marrying his daughter, under the same circumstances as are told of Peau d'âne. The same three dresses are asked for and obtained. They are, one golden like the sun, another silvery like the moon, and the third shining like the stars. The princess also obtains of her father in like manner a mantle of a thousand kinds of skins and furs. These being in her possession she determines on flight. She puts on the mantle, blackens her face and hands with soot, packs up her three dresses, together with a gold and silver spinning-wheel and a gold reel, and sets off. She reaches a forest where she sleeps all night. Next morning the king, who is hunting, rescues her from his hounds who are upon her and takes her into his service as kitchen drudge. One evening a grand ball is given. Allerleirauh (all sorts of rough), as she is called, says to the cook, "Can't I go to the door and look in?" "Yes," says he, "but come back in half-an-hour to sweep up the ashes." She goes off to her den, washes the soot off her face and hands, and puts on her sun-coloured dress. She makes a sensation at the ball, dances with the king, and flies without being perceived. She gets back to her den, blackens herself again, puts on the skin, and presents herself to the cook. He goes off to see the ball, first setting her to make the king's soup. She does so, and drops purposely the ring into it. The cook comes back and serves the soup.

---

* See Deulin (ante), p. 117, et seqq. M. Deulin translates the heroine's name very adroitly as "peau de toutes bêtes."

The king thinks it better than usual, and sends for the cook, who is obliged to own that Allerleirauh has made it. She is sent for, but discloses nothing, only says that she is good for nothing but to have boots thrown at her head (which appears to be the way in which she is ill-treated in the kitchen). A second ball comes off. Exactly the same things occur over again, the only difference being that she wears her moon-coloured robe, and puts the silver spinning-wheel into the soup. She tells the king when she is sent for that she is only fit to receive boots thrown at her head. A third ball comes off. She puts on her star-coloured robe, and dances with the king as before. This time he slips a ring on her finger, but as she outstays the half-hour she has to retreat precipitately, and has only time to put her skins over the dress, and leaves one finger unblackened. She makes the soup a third time, puts the gold reel into it, and is sent for to the king, who then perceives the white finger, and his ring upon it. He seizes her hand, and the skins that cover her fall off. An explanation then ensues, and the two are married.

In Russia, in a tale of Afanassief (the 28th of the sixth book), a young girl whose father wishes to marry her puts on a pigskin and flies, taking with her three brilliant dresses of the stars, moon, and sun, hidden in three wooden dolls. These dolls, dressed as old women, assist the fugitive to go underground, where they all enter a forest, and find near an oak a palace of a princess, who has a son young and handsome. The heroine marries the prince, and then takes off the pigskin, but not before.*

In Schleicher's *Litauische märchen* (or Lithuanian stories) a king wishes to marry his daughter-in-law, because she is the only woman who equals his late queen in beauty. She flies, but first obtains of him a mantle of pigskin, a silver dress, a diamond ring, and gold shoes.†

* De Gubernatis's *Zoologie Mythologique*, vol. i. p. 223; and vol. ii. p. 5 (French translation). The wooden doll appears in the Italian version of *Maria di legno*, published by Busk (Deulin, p. 87). I shall have occasion to quote De Gubernatis's great work again, and I must say of it that it is one of the most remarkable combinations of erudition and imagination that this age has produced.

† Deulin's *Contes de ma mère l'Oie avant Perrault*, p. 86.

In the tale of "Rashie coat," told in the lowlands of Scotland,* the heroine is a princess whom her father wishes to marry to somebody for whom she has no regard. In other respects the tale is in substance Peau d'âne combined with Cinderella's slipper. Rashie coat having become cook for the nonce, while the other servants are gone out, a fairy dresses the dinner for her to enable her to slip away to church. She goes to church in this way three times, with the same result as follows from the ball in Peau d'âne.

In the Scottish highlands is told the story of "a king who wished to marry his own daughter.† This Gaelic tale is made up, like the one just mentioned, of the incidents of Peau d'âne and Cinderella's slipper, and the attendance at the ball is exchanged for going to church. This latter circumstance, however, which as we have seen occurs also in "Rashie coat," must not be attributed to northern propriety only, for it is found also in the Russian and the Greek Cinderella.‡

These illustrations could be augmented by the text of the versions of Greece, Albania, and Spain, and by variants everywhere.§ But what I have given is quite enough to show the consensus which exists throughout all these cosmopolitan stories in regard to their main and significant features.

These illustrations have been taken from Europe only. But the first meridian of our story is much more eastward. Asia saw its birth, and its first circulation. Its parentage is a Vedic myth, afterwards embodied in the Rigveda.‖

In the eighteenth hymn of the 8th book of the Rigveda may be read the following pre-Brahmanic narrative:¶—

* *Contes populaires de la Grande Bretagne*, par Loys Bruèyre, pp. 39-41. M. Bruèyre quotes Chambers's *Popular Rhymes of Scotland*.

† Loys Bruèyre (*ante*), pp. 41-44. This is taken from Campbell's *Tales of the Western Highlands*.

‡ *Afanassief*, bk. vi. 28, and 11, 31, quoted by De Gubernatis, *Mythologic Zoologique*, vol. i. pp. 223-224. Pio's *Contes populaires Grecs*, p. 6, Σαμαρο-κουτσουλοῦ.

§ Deulin (*ante*), p. 87.

‖ Vedic myths, as distinguished from the Vedas, are older thàn the Aryan emigration. See Comparetti's *Edipo e la mitologia comparata*, p. 1.

¶ Gubernatis's *Mythologic Zoologique*, vol. ii. p. 3. See also his *Letture sopra la mitologia Vedica*, pp. 68, 69, 88, 89.

A young nymph, named Apâlâ, comes down from the mountain to draw water, and in so doing draws *soma* (or ambrosia), which she presents to the Sun God,[*] Indra, the drinker of that immortal beverage. Indra, pleased with this attention of the nymph, who, though young, is ugly and deformed, consents to pass over her head, her chest, and her stomach. She becomes purified also by the wheel of his car, the car itself and the helm of the car being passed over her, and when he has done this Indra gives her, to complete his favour, a shining robe made of the skin of the sun.

In a legend of the Brihaddevatâ the story is told thus. The same Apâlâ asks of Indra to make her a magnificent and perfect skin. Indra passes over her with the wheels, the car, and the helm three times, and by these means succeeds in removing from her the hideous skin which has covered her. Inside this skin was found a bristle ; on the outside the skin was covered with bristling hairs.[†]

Here is the common mother of all the stories which have thrown roots into the countries of Europe :—

The water which Apâlâ draws for the God, and which, because of its holy destination, becomes the *soma* on which he lives, is expressed in the soup which Zuccaccia, the Mantuan heroine, and Allerleirauh,. make for their princes. In the Irish tale it has come down to shaving water.

As Indra drives his car three times over the body of Apâlâ, her head, her chest, her stomach, so the prince raps Zuccaccia over the knees, the shoulders, and the feet with the poker, the tongs, and his riding-whip, also three times in all, while in " Il Trottolino " the same blows are inversely received by the prince from the young lady herself.[‡]

In the English tale the cook who takes the prince's place, *pro hac*

---

[*] See De Gubernatis's *Letture sopra la mitologia Vedica*, p. 190, as to Indra being sometimes considered the sun.

[†] De Gubernatis's *Mythologie Zoologique*, vol. ii. p. 4.

[‡] One of the blows has been imported into the Venetian version of Cinderella, *La Conza-senare.* Bernoni's *Fiabe e novelle popolari Veneziane*, p. 41. " He takes up the tongs and hits her on the head." (*E el ciapa la moleta, e el ghe la dà su la testa.*)

vice, breaks Catskin's head three times with the basin and her two culinary weapons. The Mantuan tale and Allerleirauh are severally in accord with Zuccaccia and Catskin. Finally Apâlâ is liberated from her own hideous skin, which, as in the Russian tale, is a pigskin, while the others doff only their more adventitious covering. And Indra, though he is not said exactly to marry the maid, makes her what looks like a wedding present.

The Vedic narratives thus contain most of the leading traits of·our European stories, and these traits are so peculiar in themselves, and so important in their bearing upon the march of the story, that to one and all there can only be a single original, viz. the Rigveda story and its adjunct.

It is quite true that these latter do not comprise all the incidents which run through the European folk-tales. There is no old king that covets his young daughter, and no flight of the latter to avoid so repulsive a union. It is true also that the three dresses which the daughter obtains from her father, and which accompany her flight, according to all the European narratives of her adventures, make no appearance in the Hindoo original. But these traits, so invariable in the other stories, though found neither in the Rigveda nor the Brihad-devatâ, must have appeared in some early Indian fiction developed from them, for they are, as we shall see, explicable only upon principles of ancient Hindoo mythology, and, being found in all or the most part of the derivative fictions of Europe, must by necessity have had a common origin, which preceded in time their respective introductions into Europe.

We may therefore assume that of the original myth there was once a form which comprehended all those points from which the European stories do not depart, and upon which their consensus has been seen to be palpable. This will give us an original myth, in which the Indian father performed his objectionable *rôle,* and in which Apâlâ, for the golden robe which Indra gave her in the Veda, received or had three dresses, recalling the three luminous heavens, for that, as we shall see, is the meaning of these habiliments and their number.

While all these stories, including the English and Irish versions,

to which I have called attention this evening, agree so materially
with each other, no matter what their present habitat be, that
they can only, as I have contended, be affiliated to some identical,
though remote parent, our two stories, as independently working out
the same fundamental ideas, differ from some of the versions in a few of
their incidents, and these special differences are not without their own
peculiar interests.   I do not allude merely to their variant mode of
stating the leading fact which compelled our English Catskin to set
out on her travels.   This alteration was doubtless a compulsory sacri-
fice to propriety made by the nurses whose audiences were confined to
the interiors of well-to-do families, and they are entitled to some
credit for their ingenuity in softening an old-world horror,* as they
must have thought it, into a plain and probable fact which their own
experiences may have taught them—the bad temper of a squire who
realised the disagreeable truth that his acres held in tail male were
slipping away to a remote cousin only because his wife would persist
in presenting him with unnecessary female heirs.

The same feeling of propriety had acted on the Irish story, though
it showed itself in a characteristically different way.   It passed
through simpler minds, and the moral feeling of the Irish peasantry
was satisfied by converting the father into the father-in-law, and the
rest of the charming tale was preserved untouched.

These two alterations, however, are the only modern things about
either the English or the Irish Catskin.   In all other respects the
two stories retain the true archaic essence of the primitive myth.
The English Catskin hides her three splendid robes in a forest, and
to that forest she repairs when she wishes to resign her temporary
splendour and re-enter her state of squalor.   The cook, to whom she
is subjected in her obscured condition, ill-treats her even to the
extent of breaking her head three times.   To remove the bloodstains
from her face and head Catskin washes herself at a crystal waterfall
in the forest.

---

* So the Greeks softened down the Œdipus saga at the expense of its force
For in some of the versions he did not marry his mother but another wife of
Laius. See Comparetti's *Edipo*, p. 37.

Though in respect of the person who inflicts the blows the English story departs from the Italian and the Hindoo forms, it is curious to observe that on this point it is quite at one with the German version. There another menial than the cook (an immaterial difference) throws boots at the heroine's head, and the prince is entirely guiltless, though, as the representative of Indra, he would only have followed suit if he had done something of the sort.

The Irish story of Catskin, perhaps the best of these fictions, while substantially true to the *motif* which governs them all, has at least one striking peculiarity of its own. The filly who comes to the aid of the puzzled princess is a far more picturesque personage than the aged female mentors of the Bear and Zuccaccia, and she is at the same time a waif of the old mythology of Ireland, where a speaking horse figures as a sort of Delphic Apollo.*

It is the filly also who must be presumed to provide the dress of catskins for her *protégée*. It is not clear how her English and Italian

---

* Before Christianity there was a zoological mythology in Ireland. Of this the *Each labhra* (or talking horse) and the royal cat of Clough, equally a speaker, were the most conspicuous members. They became mute on hearing St. Patrick's mass-bell (*Transactions of the Ossianic Society*, vol. ii. p. 37). In a tale composed in the Irish language, about the year 1725, entitled *The Son of Bad Counsel* (*ibid.* pp. 40, 41, and P. Kennedy's *Legendary Fictions of the Irish Celts*, p. 133), it is said that at Allhallows this talking horse used to emerge as far as his middle from a hill, now called Dunbin, near Dundalk, and would speak in human voice to any person that consulted him, giving oracular answers as to what should befal the inquirer between then and the same festival in the ensuing year. Mr. Nicholas O'Kearney (*Transactions of the Ossianic Society*, vol. ii. p. 41) says that "it is a popular belief in Ireland that there were horses in the olden time which were gifted with human faculties." In the Irish traditional tale of *Conn-eda, or the Golden Apples of Lough Erne*, taken down by the same gentleman from the lips of a professed story-teller, and communicated by him to the *Cambrian Journal* (vol. ii. p. 101, and *seqq.*), the hero succeeds in his adventure through the assistance of a shaggy pony, who talks as well as acts. This is a folk-tale of great interest. Besides containing elements peculiar to Irish traditional story-telling it has a good many of the general features of European folk-lore, such as the bird of knowledge (see mad D'Aulnoy's *La belle Etoile et le Prince Chéri*), the slaying of the pony and his revival as a young prince, the appeasing the serpents each with a piece of meat, the taking objects, necessary for the *dénoument*, out of the pony's ears, &c. &c. I have ventured to suggest that this tale should be transplanted from its present

sisters get their hideous coverings, but Peau d'âne, Allerleirauh, and Schleiher's Lithuanian princess, extort their disguises from their unsuspecting fathers.

The stories of Peau d'âne, Catskin, Ugly Gourd, Pigskin, Wooden Doll, All-kinds-of-rough, or by whatever name we and others elect to call the heroine, thus seem to be forms only of an Aryan pre-historic tale of almost illimitable antiquity. We have seen it in its first sketch, and we have traced it as it completed and diffused itself through time and space. But what, after all, was its meaning or object?

Is it a tale only of imaginative fiction, which by the force of its incidents and *personae* has so won upon the Aryan mind that it has for these and no other reasons established for itself a copyright in every land colonized by Aryan immigrants? Or has it any part in that fascinating lore which learned men and profound thinkers have evolved in our age, a waif of that infantile system of astronomy which the grown-up children of the early ages thought out for themselves without any precise anticipation of the Newtonian philosophy, and which the children of the present generation would, probably just as naturally, expound to each other if they never saw the governess or the professor?

If the last question is to be answered in the affirmative, our tale may be taken to be one of the most plausible of the exponents of the sun and dawn theories of Cox, De Gubernatis, and Max Müller. Without the application of this or some other esoteric view the story is certainly revolting and perhaps inexplicable.* By its invocation the incidents are blameless and easy of comprehension, provided, of course, we consent to make ourselves children for the nonce. Without this or some similar explanation it is impossible also to understand why

position, where it is overlaid and lost, to the more sympathetic pages of the *Record.* [See *Folk-Lore Record*, vol. ii. pp. 180—193.] I should observe that the horse myth is also found in a tale of a kindred race—the Gael of North Britain (see Campbell's story of *The Widow and her Daughters*, and Bruyère's *Contes populaires de la Grande Bretagne*, p. 121).

* M. Deulin (*Contes de ma mère l'Oye*, p. 83) apologises for the leading incident by suggesting that the story itself was invented before the laws of morality were yet settled. (Ce conte a dû être inventé à une epoque où les lois de la morale n'étaient pas encore fixées).

all the offshoots of the Ayran population, in all the countries through which that wave has passed in its migrations from Asia to Ireland, should have united in introducing and preserving a story so startlingly repugnant in its literal *motif.*

The probabilities of the suggested explanation may be thus stated. Amongst the early Aryans, Aurora (or dawn) was a goddess, young, handsome, and given to dancing.* She was the daughter of the old sun. Her beauty was for the time obscured by the advent of night, though it still existed even behind that veil. When, however, that obscurity was removed by the clear starlight, or the full moonlight of night, then Aurora's beauty again asserted itself, and in the short period intervening between the early dawn and the risen sun's full effulgence her beauties became more manifest until they were finally absorbed in his greater effulgence.

This young Aurora the old sun, her father, pursues, and wishes to wed, for the former Aurora, her mother, has died and left him alone. The father anticipates that the new dawn will equal in beauty the one which is gone. This is the theory, and we have only to see if it can be approximated to our stories—one and all of them.

Most of the stories agree with each other in the statements that the old king, who has had a beautiful wife, is enchanted to find that the daughter is as beautiful as the lost mother. They also equally agree in the statement that he pursues the daughter with the same solicitations which he had before addressed to the mother.

This means that to the old personified sun, who is leaving this world, the new Aurora, who will be the same as the past one, seems as gorgeously beautiful as was the Aurora of the previous morning. He pursues her therefore as he had pursued the other, but not with the same success.

The Aurora of the future, who is not to be for him, flies, and is lost in the forest, or is shut up in a frame of wood, i. e., in Vedic language, she is enveloped in the total obscurity of night.†

* De Gubernatis's *Letture sopra la mitologia*, pp. 57, 66 (saltatrice).

† As to this meaning of forest and wooden covering, see De Gubernatis's *Introduzione* to the *Novelline di Santo Spirito*, p. 12. See his *Letture, ante*, p. 94.

The heroine's travestiment of hideous clothing is an intensification of that darkness, and when the Irish Catskin stains her face, her arms, and her hands with a brown dye, the idea of darkness is meant to be further augmented. But the passage of Aurora through the dim obscure, still taking her to be as ontological as ourselves, is brightened by intervals of splendour. It is in this sense that our heroine puts on her three brilliant dresses. We have seen that in Peau d'âne's case these are sky-coloured, moon-coloured, and sun-coloured. Two of Zuccaccia's are air-coloured, bestrewn with the stars of the heavens, and sea-water-coloured, with gold fishes swimming about; while the third is interwoven with little bells and chains of gold. In the Mantuan story two of the dresses are like the moon and the sun, and the third is bestrewn with gems. The Irish Catskin's are of silk and silver thread, of silk and gold thread, and silk with diamonds and pearls. Two of Allerleirauh's are of gold like the sun, of silver like the moon, while the third is shining like the stars. Afanassief's Russian heroine has three dresses precisely like those of Allerleirauh.

Quaint as all this is, its meaning is not far to seek. The three dresses of Peau d'âne, Zuccaccia and her sister of Mantua, the Russian heroine, the Irish Catskin, and Allerleirauh, represent the three luminous states of the heavens, viz. where the moon is seen, where the stars are seen, where the sun is risen. And it is mostly in this order of rotation that each heroine dons them. The last wearing immediately precedes her own absorption by the new sun, her lover and husband. Even the English Catskin, though her dresses are not specified, puts on her most brilliant one last of all, as we are particularly told in the poem.

Zuccaccia's robe of sea-water with gold fishes swimming in it is Vedic as much as the others, for night is called ocean in the Rigveda.*

The fountain at which Peau d'âne washes the soot off her face, the crystal waterfall in which the English Catskin removes her blood-stains, represent the dew of the early morn.

The cook who strikes the same Catskin, the menial who buffets Aller-

---

* See De Gubernatis's *Introduzione* to the *Novelline di Santo Spirito* p. 12 ; also his *Mythologic Zoologique*, vol. ii. p. 176.

leirauh, are Vedic monsters of the night, types of its dangers and inflictions.*

The removal of the deforming disguises—ass's skin, catskin, pig-skin, wooden case, or stale gourd peelings—is the full apparition of the lovely dawn of the south, when all darkness has disappeared.

The marriage of the heroine to the prince is the absorption of the dawn into the triumphant glories of the sunlit day.

If all this is meant in the Vedic tale of Apâlâ and Indra—and the learned think so,† it must also be meant in our two tales of Catskin and their sister stories of the rest of Europe, for they all are but a reflexion of that primæval myth.

But, whatever be the meaning of all these quaint and self-resembling stories, my object this evening has, I think, been accomplished. I have shown, I trust, what Goldsmith's allusion really was, viz. to a version, English or Irish, of this enormously ancient and ubiquitous fiction, and I have shown also, what had been forgotten, viz. that both are still in existence.

Since the above was written our Honorary Secretary, Mr. G. L. Gomme, F.S.A., has kindly lent me his copy of "Ancient Poems, Ballads, and Songs of the Peasantry of England, taken down from oral recita tion, and transcribed from private manuscripts, rare broadsides, and scarce publications, by James Henry Dixon. Edited by Robert Bell." (London: John Parker and Son, West Strand. 1857.) At pp. 115-122 of this collection is a ballad in five parts, entitled " The Wandering young Gentlewoman, or Catskin." The compiler (or the editor) says of it :—" The following version of this ancient English ballad has been collated with three copies. In some editions it is called *Catskin's Garland; or, the Wandering Young Gentlewoman*. * * * For some account of it see *Pictorial Book of Ballads*, ii. 153, edited by Mr. S. Moore." This " Catskin's Garland " is another poetic version of our tale, more rude and popular than that of Mr. Halliwell-Phillipps,

---

* De Gubernatis's *Letture*, p. 42.

De Gubernatis says : " Una fanciulla di nome Apâlâ che io sospetto asser la nostra Aurora," *Letture sopra la mitologia Vedica*, p. 68.

and in different metre. There are some differences of detail also, but they are only slight. In Mr. Hill's ballad the cook is kind to Catskin. It is the young gentleman's mother that strikes her with the ladle and the skimmer, and throws the basinful of water in her face, and it is her father who, hearing of her marriage, goes and finds her out in the disguise of a beggar.

> Who hearing his daughter was married so brave,
> He said, "In my noddle a fancy I have ;
> Dressed like a poor man now a journey I'll make,
> And see if she on me some pity will take."

In all probability another English version still *de facto* exists in the heart of London, however little hope there be of its ever coming to light. I mean the version once prevailing in our metropolis, which until twenty years ago was bought and sold in Seven Dials. My knowledge of this curious fact is of very recent date.

Towards the end of last February a feeling of prevision took me to Monmouth Court, Seven Dials, to the shop of Mr. W. S. Fortey, printer and publisher of what literature still survives in that somewhat unsavoury locality, and there I learnt what follows :—

Thirty years ago his house took over from Mr. Pitt, a printer of the neighbouring Little St. Andrew Street, his business, his copyrights, and his unsold stock. Our re-discovered Catskin was amongst the latter, and the new purchasers continued to print and sell her story until about twenty years ago, when the public demand flickered and its re-production ceased. Old narrative poetry of this sort had been superseded by more appetizing pabulum. A similarly once popular ballad, called the *Fish and the Ring*, shared the same fate at the same time. Since that epoch Catskin has never been set up. She and her old-world sister, still unsold, were relegated to the obscurity of a garret in Monmouth Court, and there they are. "It would take three or four whole days to look them through," said Mr. Fortey, "and without that looking through there would be no chance of finding Catskin." Her ballad, I further learnt, was a little (penny) book, adorned with four woodcuts, perhaps one to each canto. One of these cuts was still agreeably fresh in Mr. Fortey's memory, for the recollection made him mirthful even in the gloom of a wet afternoon in February.

In this cut Catskin sat nursing her cat. Does not this latter circumstance look like a special feature peculiar to the London version? This cut may be Catskin's fairy adviser, and through her mysterious agency may have come the feline cloak, which has given a lasting name to the heroine. I found Mr. Fortey pleasant and intelligent, but firm in maintaining the inaccessibility of his stores—a resolution the more to be regretted as they promise much to the Folk-Lorist.

HENRY CHARLES COOTE.

BIOGRAPHICAL MYTHS;

ILLUSTRATED FROM THE LIVES OF BUDDHA AND MUHAMMAD.

[Read at the Meeting of the Society on 9 February, 1880.]

IT is a familiar fact to students of history that in the course of ages accretions of a mythological nature gather round historical personages, until these become so overlaid with incrustations from fairyland that they are indistinguishable from the creations of pure fiction. In such case historians are wont to regard the accretions as of little or no consequence, testifying for the most part only to the credulity of the multitude, and at best only useful for some germ of historic event which they may contain.

But another view may be taken of these mythic accretions. It may be that these stories which fill so completely the biographies of the heroes of antiquity do not fall into their places by chance, nor take their shape by accident, but on the contrary gather round their object according to law, and are fashioned by influences which, divergent in outward seeming, are everywhere alike. Limits of time will not permit of the inductive building-up of this theory, and I will accordingly so far presume as to state the theory first, and afterwards deductively explain its illustrations.

An " historic person," that is, a person in and by himself, is a very different being from the " person in history," that is, the man as he appears to his disciples or followers. Personally, a great man may have failings, weaknesses, peculiarities; but these for the most part do not appear in his public career, and such of them as do, appear to a great extent transformed. For a great man is always idealised by his followers. He fills for them the void, he supplies the want of the age. For years, possibly for generations, men have looked for him;

they have formed conceptions more or less definite of what he will be; lofty and perhaps wild expectations of what he will do. Thus a great man finds when he comes an ideal already existing in men's minds, and all his actions are viewed through this mental lens. He becomes in men's eyes the actual objective embodiment of what had previously existed subjectively in the mind. And yet he exercises a modifying influence upon the ideal he fulfils. For he must of necessity "live and move and have his being" arising out of his own personal bias, and of equal necessity the ideal must be modified to correspond with the reality. So that by the time his career has ended, and his portrait is indelibly stamped upon the minds of his followers, that portrait is one, not of the ideal which was his precursor, not of the person himself with all his little idiosyncrasies (the "historic person" as I termed him,) but the person viewed through the medium of the ideal, a being that has grown up out of the subjective ideal modified by the objective reality, or what for distinction's sake I have ventured to call "the person in history."

This process in the mind of a body of persons is, indeed, exactly analogous to that which takes place in the mind of an individual when he sees acted, for instance, a play which he has previously much read and studied. As we read and study we form, if we possess any imaginative power, an ideal conception of the characters; we modify and improve that conception at our will, and each successive reading in some way modifies the ideal. But when once we have seen the play acted we can no longer do that. Henceforth the basis of our vision is the acting we have seen with the outward eye. And yet not the actual objective acting, but the acting as interpreted by our previous ideal. For ever after, therefore, the play has for us an objective and a subjective aspect blended together; the subjective admitting in itself of an infinite expansion, but controlled and limited by the objective. Such, it seems to me, is the great man; neither his own individuality, nor his ideal, but a combination of the two. And this composite being is the truly historical one. It is neither the man nor the ideal, but both together, which form the cosmic force we see acting in history.

When once an ideal exists, it may be illustrated, magnified, ennobled, exaggerated to the highest degree. Stories of olden time, scraps of folk-lore, the orphan waifs and strays of mythology, find ready welcome under the sheltering wing of an expansive ideal. Even though they be mutually contradictory, they are easily reconciled. But, so soon as the ideal receives an historical fulfilment, there is an immediate and necessary change. The stories have now to undergo a struggle for existence. All of them that are out of harmony with the historical fulfilment immediately fall away. Others of a neutral tint receive a new colouring. Others again find in the history new points to which to adhere. So that, though the body of myths may continue, it is strangely transformed from one lawless and incoherent into one ruled by a law of conformity to the fulfilled ideal.

If the portrait of a great man in history arises in such a way as this, then the biographical myths connected with him become of importance. We know, in the abstract, that great men are creatures of the times which they themselves help to modify. It is by the study of the myths of their lives that we learn both what the times were and what influence the great men have had upon them. For, on the one hand, by tracing back the myths to the great body from whence they come, we may arrive at some notion of the ideal which preceded the hero; and, on the other hand, by observing the modifications which the myths have undergone we may obtain some knowledge of the man himself in history, as he appeared to his followers and contemporaries. This theory I will now endeavour to illustrate from the biographies of those eminent men, Buddha and Muhammad.

Corresponding, presumably, to the unity of human nature, it seems that myths, though they attach themselves to any convenient point, yet cluster most thickly around four periods of a great man's life, viz.:—

    I. *Birth;* when the child shows precocious signs of his future greatness;

    II. *Early manhood;* when, passing from the passivity of childhood, his predestined course begins to awaken within him;

    III. *Mature manhood;* when the impulse reaches its culminating point, and the full-grown man enters upon his career;

    IV. *Death;* when the results of his life are visited with a fitting end.

These four cycles appear, more or less broken, in all the cases I have examined. In Buddha and Muhammad they are almost perfect, and in these, moreover, we can trace the formation of the cycle.

Before Buddha is born, the queen his mother has a dream " in which she thought she saw a six-tusked white elephant, his head coloured like a ruby, descend thro' space," and the sight gave her such joy as she had never known before.* The interpretation given by the Rishis is:—

> . . . .
> If the mother, in her dream, behold
> A white elephant, ...
> That mother, when she bears a son,
> Shall bear one chief of all the world,
> Able to profit all flesh;
> Able to save and deliver the world and men
> From the deep sea of misery and grief.†

The birth itself is accompanied by remarkable manifestations of nature. "Do you not observe," says the messenger to the king's ministers, " how the great earth is rocking as a ship borne over the waves? And see how the sun and moon are darkened. And see how all the trees are blossoming as if the season had come . . . . tho' there be no clouds, yet the soft rain is falling, and the air is moved by a gentle and cool breeze—hark to the sound of that voice of Brahma, so sweetly melodious in the air," &c. &c.‡

Then, amid wondrous things which one has not time to relate, " the child, being born, said these words: ' No further births have I to endure! this is my very last body! now shall I attain to the condition of Buddha!' Then, without aid, standing on the ground, he walked seven steps, whilst lotus flowers sprang up beneath his feet, and in perfectly rounded accents he said, ' Among all creatures I am the most excellent, for I am about to destroy and extirpate the roots of sorrow caused by the universal evil of birth and death.' " §

Now let us cross from India to Arabia. Amina, the mother of Muhammad, had also a dream; but the dream interpreted itself.

* Beal, Romantic Legend of Sakya Buddha, 37.
† Ibid. 38.　　　　　　　　　　　‡ Ibid. 45 f.
§ Ibid. 47.

" Knowest thou," the vision said, " whom thou art to bear?" " No, I do not," replied Amina: "thou shalt bear," answered the vision, " the Lord and Prophet of thy people." *   Amina was encircled by a brilliant light which shone over the whole east; and when the little Muhammad was born " he placed his little hands upon the earth and lifted up his head toward heaven." †   Blessings, too, he spread around him.   Halyma, Muhammad's nurse, says that the year she received him was dry and barren; there was no milk for the children, none for the flocks and herds.   But on the advent of the infant Prophet milk flowed in abundance, and the lands of the Banû Sâd, usually arid and parched, were rich and fruitful.‡   Nor were the wonders confined to the Prophet's own people.   Jews, Christians, and Infidels—all heard in ways more or less notable of Muhammad's birth.   " I was a youth of seven or eight years old," says Hassan b. Thâbit, " when one day a Jew ascended a watch-tower in Madîna, and cried as loud as he could: 'O Jews! O Jews!'   They crowded round and said: 'What is it?'   He answered and said : 'This night the star of Ahmad has arisen, this night he has been born.' " §

The identity of motive in these two groups is apparent.   In each there appears the marvellous heralding, the precocious indications of future eminence, the tokens in nature of the advent of a hero.   But the ideal, common to both, has been modified in its expression according to the circumstances of each people.   The words put into the mouth of the infant Buddha are, like the prayer of the young Muhammad, suitable alone to the genius of the respective men.   So too nature spontaneously puts forth her glory on Buddha's birth; and this is entirely in accordance with Buddhist sentiment, which acknowledges no controlling power beyond nature.   With Muhammad, on the contrary, the prophet's power, or the divine power accompanying him, controls nature; and in this is reflected the Semitic view of nature. Indeed, if one transposes the myths, and imagines Muhammad talking of his innate power to save, or Buddha praying to a divine being, imagines elephants in the plains of Arabia, or flocks and herds in the

---

* Sprenger, Das Leben u. die Lehre des Mohammad, i. 142.

† Sprenger, u. s. i. 164.   ‡ Sprenger, u. s. i. 162-3.

§ Sprenger, u. s. i. 175.

palace gardens of Magadha, one sees how entirely the realisation of the ideal has been determined by local causes.

As Buddha grew up to manhood he meditated upon human suffering and misery, and little by little his ideas grew clear. And simultaneously the myths again cluster into what I have termed the *cycle of early manhood.* As Buddha sits in contemplation under a tree, some holy Rishis, who are flying through space (as holy men are wont to do in India), find themselves restrained by some' unseen force; and the shadow of the tree, far from changing with the revolution of the sun, remains as a fixed shelter over Buddha's head.* The unfailing signs of a Budda, the 32 marks of a perfect man, begin to appear upon his body. "There formed on his forehead, between his eyes, a circle of hair, from which was constantly emitted a flood of light, whilst his hands and his feet were so admirably proportioned, and the fingers and toes so beautifully connected together as by a network filament, that his very appearance was enough to convert and restrain all who beheld him."† On his foot appears the "thousand radiated wheel," the sign *par excellence* of a Buddha, and the print whereof may be seen in Siam to this day. It would occupy one's whole time to enumerate, not to say dilate upon, all the marvels that surround Buddha's youth; it must suffice to say that much of the imagery is traceable to old mythologic stories of some solar hero, which gradually gathered around the ideal Buddha, and have now clustered around the facts which accompanied the development on this earth of Gautama Sakya Mûni.

Turning to Muhammad, we shall find that an identical motive—the desire to keep in mind the early development of the prophet—has taken peculiarly Semitic shape. One day, when he was a youth, himseemed there came to him "two, one on the earth, and one between heaven and earth . . . . . . And one said to the other, cut out his heart. They cut open my body and took out my heart. They took away the devil's part of it and a clot of blood and threw these two things away. They washed my heart; and one asked the other for the shakînah, which was of a dazzling white. It was laid in my heart ; then they closed up my body, and stamped the ' seal of a

* Beal, *u. s.* 75-78.   † Beal, *u. s.* 179.

prophet' between my shoulders." And then, when he was twenty years old, a monk met him on a journey and observed every stone and tree bow to him, and saw also the 'seal of a prophet,' "which looked like an apple." * Moreover he too is shadowed from the heat, but it is by two angels who constantly hover round him.

In this group, even more clearly than in the birth group, can be seen how an ideal, identical both in Arabia and India, took a shape determined by the external conditions of its realisation. The signs of a perfect man which mark Buddha are precisely parallel to the cleansing of Muhammad's heart; the thousand-rayed wheel on Buddha's foot expresses to the Hindu exactly what the prophetic seal on Muhammad's shoulder does to the Arab. The thought is the same, the expression could not fail to be different.

We now come to the *cycle of mature manhood*. The attainment of perfect knowledge is preceded in Buddha's life by a terrible struggle with Mâra, the demon of evil. All the incarnate demons of lust and gratification crowd around Buddha, and endeavour by allurements and threats to turn him from his purpose. But in vain. Sitting calmly under the bodhi tree, he attained to full enlightenment, and the response of nature is given in eloquent words which I cannot refrain from quoting: "At this time the heavens, the earth, and all the spaces between the encircling zones of rock, were lit up with a supernatural splendour; whilst flowers and every kind of precious perfume fell down in thick profusion around Bhagavat, who had now attained perfect enlightenment ; and, whilst the earth shook six times, the Devas sang together in the midst of space a joyous song, and rained down upon earth every kind of sweet flower . . . There was no ill-feeling or hatred in the hearts of men; but whatever want there was, whether of food, or drink, or raiment, was at once supplied; the blind received their sight, the deaf heard, and the dumb spake. Those who were bound in hell were released ; and every kind of being—beasts, demons, and all created things—found rest and peace." †

With Muhammad the Kuran is of course the great seal of his prophetic mission. Nevertheless there exists a tradition (that of his ascent into heaven) "which," says Dr. Sprenger, "is for the Moslims

* Sprenger, *u. s.* i. 167.   † Beal, *u. s.* 224, 225.

what the resurrection of Christ is for us: the noblest and all-sufficient proof of his mission. They are right. While the legends of the boyhood depict the ideal of a prophet in his contact with mankind, and are at the same time preparatory, the Ascent into Heaven shows us his relation to the spiritual world and lets us view his divine con-secration. The Ascent into Heaven is the completion of the Moslim 'Evangelium Infantiae.' "* I will not enter upon the details of this famous but perhaps tedious legend, which relates how Muhammad passed thro' the seven heavens, saluting in turn the saints of the older dispensations; then receiving from the throne of God fifty daily prayers for his people; getting them gradually reduced at the sugges-tion of Moses, till for very shame he could ask no more; and finally coming away with the five daily prayers that Muhammadans still use. I wish rather to note how the groups of legends, having the same ideal, diverge consistently in expression, each group following the tradition of its hero's life. Let me also draw attention to Dr. Sprenger's words, and to their agreement with the theory I have laid down. Indeed if the Mi'raj, or " Ascent into Heaven," is the comple-tion of the Muhammadan " Gospel of the Infancy," then the Buddhist " Gospel of the Infancy " finds its completion in the scene under the bodhi tree.

Its completion, perhaps, in a strange sense. For, passing to the *Cycle of Death*, the curious fact has to be noticed, that of the six versions of which I have been able to consult translations,—viz. the Sanskrit, Tibetan, Chinese, Siamese, Burmese, and Singhalese,—only two, the Burmese and Singhalese, contain an account of Buddha's death. Of the others, the Tibetan and Sanskrit, purporting to have been orally delivered by Buddha, might not unreasonably be supposed to be imperfect, but so much cannot be said for the great Chinese and Siamese versions. And this fact is doubly curious when we remember that if Buddha lived he must unquestionably have died. I do not know that any explanation has hitherto been offered of this feature; but my theory enables me to offer an explanation which I will submit for what it may be worth. Death does not present to the Buddhist that sharp line of severance between soul and body, between this life

* Sprenger, *u. s.* iii. lvi.

and the next, that it does to us. It is simply a transition from this state
of being into another, to be followed probably by many more transitions
into yet other stages. And so he looks upon it as an ordinary event,
in no respect the opening of the last scene of life's tragedy. Especially
is this so in the case of Buddha himself. For Buddha had already
attained perfect enlightenment, and might be said to have already
entered Nirvâna. His life was consummated under the bodhi tree;
what followed was simply the dissolution of the atoms of his body, a
matter of comparatively small moment, and certainly fraught with no
important consequences to himself or others. Hence, it seems to me,
the necessary impulse to aggrandisement would be absent. And it so
happens that the two legends of Buddha's death, are, for legends, the
most matter-of-fact things imaginable. They admit, indeed, the very
prosaic circumstance that Buddha died of eating pork—and bad pork
too. Now Bishop Bigandet mentions that in olden times this pork
episode was a stone of offence to good Buddhists, who were sorely
satirised thereupon by the unbelieving Brahmins. Accordingly the
legend in Burmese has been so far aggrandised as to make it appear
that the pork was very good pork, and would have had no evil effects
had it not been the predestined cause of Buddha's decease. Is it too
much to suppose that the absence of the legend in the other versions
is due to a popular feeling that it had no place in the Master's
biography, which fitly closed with the episode of perfect enlightenment?

With Muhammad the case is different. Here the history has so far
conditioned the ideal as to render impossible legends of his being
taken up into heaven, or of his burial in some hidden spot; yet Dr.
Sprenger is able to give no less than seven groups of myths about the
prophet's death. The more important are these: "In the year before
his death Muhammad had constantly in his lips (by command of the
angel Gabriel) such ejaculations as 'To the praise and glory of God.
Forgive me my sins, for thou art the merciful and forgiving.' In the
month of Ramadhân of each year Gabriel used to collate the Kuran
with him; this year he collated it twice, whence Muhammad concluded
that he should not live out the year. He was not taken away un-
ceremoniously like common men, but was allowed to choose between

life and death; and, when he expressed his wish to die, the angel of death waited on him respectfully to know when he might be permitted to take the prophet's soul.* These myths," says Dr. Sprenger, " are popular and are related with great beauty." With Muhammad, therefore, the series is complete.

We have now followed Hindu and Arab from the cradle to the grave; and have seen that at the four critical periods of their career myths have clustered together with a motive identical in both cases, but necessarily and consistently divergent in colouring. I will now take a single myth from each life and try to examine more minutely how it has grown into its present shape.

The myth from Muhammad is that of the cleansing of his heart. Dr. Sprenger's account of its origin is, as far as it goes, so clear, that I do not hesitate to quote it. " In the beginning of his mission Muhammad confessed that he himself had been in error (Kur. 93, 7), but declared that God had opened his heart (Kur. 94, 1). This figurative expression was the starting-point of the fiction. The first expression was, therefore, ' The breast of the prophet was opened, and God cleansed his heart.' . . . But it was always a stumbling block that the prophet should have been in error, and the purification of his heart was transferred more and more into his youth, at first to his twentieth year; but there was no meaning in that. Then in the beginning of the eleventh; that was better, because at that date responsibility begins. Finally into his childhood." †

The ideas of orientals respecting subjective and objective are very different from ours; and to people accustomed to hear, without doubting, of visions and miracles, the story I gave a few minutes ago would not seem at all unhistorical. There can be no doubt that subjectively the prophet passed through such an experience, and in Dr. Sprenger's words we have the story of its idealisation and of its transition from one period to another of the prophet's history, until it fitted in with the general conception his people formed of him. Here, then, we see an actual historical fact idealised. But why should this particular fact have been seized on rather than any other? Because the " heart " is to the Arab, as to the Hebrew, the seat of the emotions and thoughts;

* Sprenger, u. s. iii. lv.   † Ibid. u. s. i. 168f.

before anything pure can proceed from it, it must be cleansed from all stain of sin. Not to dwell upon this point, I will only remind you that the three greatest prophets of the Hebrews, Ezekiel, Jeremiah, and Isaiah, had their hearts or lips touched by Jehovah; and that one of the most eloquent of Isaiah's writings is the passage where he describes how " one of the seraphims flew unto me, having a live coal in his hand, and he laid it upon my mouth and said: ' Lo, this hath touched thy lips; and thine iniquity is taken away, and thy sin purged.' " * It is no great stretch of imagination to suppose that some such feeling as this was current among the followers of Muhammad ; and, being current, we can see how easily it would fit itself into and idealise an historical fact, which without that would have remained a mere casual incident.

It is the great value of Muhammad's life that in it we can see this process going on; we can see the ideal floating in men's minds, coming into contact with an historical event, and watch the two together growing up into what is really the true account of the matter:—that to the people of his day Muhammad was one whose soul in infancy had been purified by God that he might be enabled to utter God's revelation. With Buddha it is otherwise. There is no independent historical tradition of him. So entirely has mythology overgrown him, that there is no difficulty in explaining him away entirely as a solar myth. And there is so much that is undoubtedly borrowed from solar legends; so much of popular folk-lore that surrounds him, that to doubt Buddha's historical existence is very pardonable. And yet, luxuriant as is this growth of legend, it is everywhere dominated by the peculiar features of Buddha's doctrine. Of this a striking instance occurs, not in the story of Buddha himself but in the story of Yasada, an early convert of Buddha's, and one whose history is very fully narrated in the Chinese gospel.

There is nothing unusual in the passage of a myth from one spot or person to another; but in such cases it is usually the details that are altered while the motive remains. That is the first principle of the school of comparative mythology. It was by this common motive that Sir George Cox traced the story of the Volsungs in the Achilleis

* Isaiah, vi. 6, 7,

of Greece and the poems of the Rig Veda. And, when single myths are transplanted into foreign soil, it is usually the germ which remains unaltered while the details change, as in the weird version of the Immaculate Conception which is found in the Finnish epic. But in the story of Yasada the exact converse takes place; while every detail is preserved, the motive is entirely changed.

As I read the story you will no doubt recognise the details of a popular folk-story, while the argument of it is essentially Buddhistic.

" Not far from the city of Benares there was, amongst other trees, a certain Nyagrodha tree, remarkable for its luxuriant growth. This tree was an object of veneration to all the people, rich and poor, who dwelt in the neighbourhood; all of whom, at certain seasons of the year, came to offer gifts and religious worship to it. And it came to pass, that, whatever prayer or vows a man made whilst in the act of worship, the same was certain to be granted. But the fact was that the previous Karma of the worshipper was the sole cause of the fulfilment of his prayer; yet men, not regarding this, attributed it entirely to the tree, and so continued to frequent the spot to offer up their prayers and present their offerings. From this circumstance, the tree was known as the ' Divine tree which granted all that was asked of it.' Now a certain nobleman had no child, and his friends advised him to pray to the ' divine tree.' Naturally, as a good Buddhist, he declined to betake himself to any such refuge. But, being finally overcome by the entreaties of his friends, he addressed the following naïve prayer to the tree: ' You tree! I have heard from certain persons that you have the power of granting the request of those who pay you religious worship! I would have you know therefore, that, if you will procure for me the birth of a well-favoured man-child, I will offer you every kind of offering, and pay you becoming veneration; but, if you cannot procure for me this boon, then I will cut you down, and root you up and utterly destroy you, and scatter the very ashes remaining after you are burnt till you are utterly annihilated and put clean out of remembrance.'

"At this fearful imprecation the Deva of the tree was immensely terrified. ' What power have I,' he said, ' to give this man a child ? All that depends upon his previous conduct and the destiny attaching to him from his former works. And yet men persist in saying that this tree, in which from old times I have taken my residence, has the power to do this or that, and if I do not give him a child he threatens to burn down my abode. Alas! Alas!' Hereupon he went to the King of the Gods and laid his sad case before him and asked him to devise some expedient by which the desire of the nobleman might be gratified. Equally with the Deva, the King of the Gods repudiated any power to interfere with the nobleman's destiny: 'but fear not,' he said, 'I will see what the character of his destiny is.' As it happened, it was the nobleman's destiny to have the child; so the Deva went down with this message: 'Go and tell that nobleman that his prayer is answered! he shall have a son.' And so all ended happily, as all should end in a fairy tale." *

The translator of this story has noted that it records the contact of the old tree-worship with Buddhist ideas. It is evident that in its details this story is one of the large class of tales in which the aid of trees, fishes, and animals is constantly invoked, and belongs with them to an early period of culture. On the other hand, the Buddhist doctrine has so permeated it as almost to nullify the earlier faith which originated it. It is on this fact that I wish to lay emphasis. While I have been speaking about ideals, and pointing out from Muhammad's life how an ideal brings into prominence what would otherwise have been mere incidental circumstances, it may have occurred to some that the ideal entirely overweighed the historical. Here, on the contrary, we see the historical controlling the ideal. And, when we remember the immense tenacity with which folk-tales of this class survive in the midst of a higher culture, we can estimate the magnitude of the force exerted by Buddha's doctrine to change so entirely the character of the birth-story of Yasada.

Here I must pause. The subject is by no means exhausted. I should like to have discussed other examples of similar cycles more or less perfect; to have examined how far personages purely mythological (so far as we know) are subject to the same law, and whether there is any criterion of distinction between them and historical personages; to have traced famous myths, like that of the "deserted babe," from

* Beal, u. s. 258ff.

Sargon of Agane in Assyria to Romulus in Italy, and from Romulus to Kullerwo in the Kalevala. I should like, too, to have inquired how far the ideal four cycles are themselves controlled by law. When we recollect the childish precocity of men of genius like Pascal and Watt; the period of meditation and spiritual awakenment which preceded the discovery of America and the writing of the " Pilgrim's Progress ;" the superhuman concentration of energy upon a single work, which by the forcible clearance of the Long Parliament changed the face of English history, and by the production of the " Essay on the Development of Christian Doctrine " changed the greatest of living Englishmen from a parish priest to a Cardinal of Rome; the final flash of intellectual fire which has made the dying utterances of Wolsey and Goethe household words among us—when we recollect how the mythic cycles are thus only the reflex of human life, we cannot resist the conclusion that the creation of these ideals is governed by the same law as the development of human nature itself.

JOHN FENTON.

STORIES FROM MENTONE.

I HEARD these stories in the Spring of 1879 from an elderly native woman who has always lived in Mentone. She told them almost wholly in the local dialect, her usual speech, and her knowledge of French or Italian being very small. On returning to my house I wrote them at the time just as she gave them, as nearly as I could remember, but turning some of them into English and some into French.

THE CHARCOAL BURNERS.

There were two poor charcoal burners who lived in the same cabin up in the hills, and they carried their charcoal to the neighbouring town for sale. One day, it being the eve of the feast of Saint John the Baptist, who was the patron saint of one of them, Baptiste told his companion that he would not work the next morning until he had done his duty in hearing mass. The other, finding him asleep at the usual hour for rising, and remembering what he had said, went off and left him. Baptiste soon arose, attended mass, and went to town with his load, meeting his friend, already well on his way home. It was nightfall before he himself started to return. With the darkness there arose so violent a storm that he was forced to seek refuge in the hollow trunk of a walnut tree.* Presently he heard the sound of voices, and he found that a party of witches were drawing near, among whom was the devil himself. In great fear and haste he scrambled up the tree as high as he could, and hid himself to the utmost among

---

* The walnut tree is believed at Mentone to be the witches' tree, and unsafe to sleep under.

the leaves. The witches stopped under the tree, where they had evidently come for a Sabbat. They began by telling one another of the deviltries each had done since last they met, how one had caused a man to die, how another had in mischief overthrown a fine olive-tree. But suddenly a witch cried out, "I surely smell a Christian, there must be one near by." They then looked in the hole, and all over the neighbourhood, but found no one. They finally concluded that doubtless some one had lately been in the hole, and had gone on his way. Soon another cried out, "But where is Ranghetta?" Ranghetta, as her name shows, was a cripple, and she was the most cunning and wicked of them all. After a while she came and excused her lateness, for the reason that she had been very busy. All were eager to hear her story, and she was about to tell them when she, too, was startled by the same smell. After having been quieted in the same way she let them know how she had just bewitched the king's only son. "I have sucked all the marrow from out his bones; he has wasted away to a skeleton, and to-morrow he will die. The marrow I put in an earthen jar, which I hid safely under the staircase in the stable, and the only cure is to rub the marrow over him, but no one can possibly find it." Baptiste heard all, and was lucky enough not to be seen. He watched the witches dance, and towards dawn they went, and he was able to come down. He sped at once in all haste to the town, found the jar of marrow, and hurried with it to the palace, where he asked to be allowed to speak with the king. The lady who came to the door, seeing an ill-clad man, black with coal, bade him begone, for they could not look after beggars when every one in the palace was busy about the dying prince. He told her that he would cure him, and was so earnest that she at last went to the king. "Never mind his ill-looks," said the king, "the best doctors in my kingdom have given the boy up, so there can be no harm in trying this man." He was then led into a great room, where thirty or forty doctors were assembled, and where lay the sick boy. He rubbed the marrow over his wasted body, and very soon he who was at his last gasp began to revive, spoke, and declared himself much better. In a few days he was out of danger. The king, filled with joy and gratitude, said to the coal-burner, " As I have but one son I adopt you for my second." So he caused him to be dressed in fine clothes, gave him a room in the palace, and made him his companion. One day riding in the country Baptiste met his former associate, and, not at all spoiled by his sudden good fortune, he greeted him cordially, without, however, being recognised until after he had told him who he was. The other was anxious to learn how he had been so fortunate, but Baptiste, unwilling to keep the king waiting, agreed to tell him the next day at the palace. The coal-burner came and heard, and went home filled with envy, and secretly determined to try his luck too at the walnut tree. Accordingly, one night he climbed up into it, and soon the witches appeared. But unfortunately he was not, like Baptiste, a pious man, nor had he been to mass that day, nor many a day before. The witches soon noticed the Christian smell, and, hunting about, found the poor man. They called him down, but he would not come; in a moment they overthrew the tree, clutched the unhappy wretch, and tossed him about until he was dead.

THE STRANGE JOURNEY.

" A friend of my parents who lived in Mentone had a sweetheart who was a witch. One hot summer night when cooling himself by the sea-side he lay down in a boat and there fell asleep. He was awoke by the sound of voices, and he saw that a party of seven witches were about to enter the boat. He hid under the bow, and the witches having seated themselves within began to sing : " Row for six, row for seven." " But the boat does not move," cried they. " There must be more than seven of us," said one. Said another, " Perhaps one is with child." " Row for eight or row for ten," then cried they all, and off went the boat. The next morning the young man found himself at Milan in a great public square, and watched by bull-dogs. He was taken back to Mentone in the same strange manner, and on the way he managed to cut a bit from the skirt of one of the witches without being seen. The day after his return on meeting his sweetheart he saw that her skirt wanted this very piece, and to her great alarm he gave it back to her. She charged him to tell no one of his adventure, under threat of great misfortune, and to ensure his secrecy she loaded him with money and other presents so that he became very rich."*

THE BEWITCHED MILL.

There was once a poor but industrious miller, and he kept his mill at work night and day in order to make both ends meet. At last came a time when a witch made up her mind to ruin him. She would manage without being seen to dip her hands in a pot of oil and then grease the wheels so that they could not turn. This she used to do when he was napping. When he was awake she would take the shape of a beautiful little red dog and fawn upon him, so that he became very fond of her and allowed her to stay at the mill. He racked his brains uselessly to find out what was wrong, and was slowly ruining himself in paying the millwrights who were always there trying to make the mill run. At last he bethought himself that there might be foul play at night during his sleep, so he determined to watch. That evening he settled himself as if for his nap, and the little dog placed herself as usual by his side waiting for his sleeping to be at mischief. He presently feigned to snore, and she, misled, stole off noiselessly to the machinery and stopped it. The miller darted quickly forward and caught her by the neck. She begged hard to be let go, or at least that the miller would change one hand for the other under the pretence of easing her pain, believing that this movement would give her a chance to escape. But the miller refused, saying, " I stir not hand nor foot till thou tell'st who thou art," and he held her tightly with the same hand until the morning angelus, when he found that he was holding a woman by the long hair of her head. " Yes," she confessed, " I am a witch who has come all the way from the Indies to torment you."

* This story is imperfect apparently, but thus it was told.

THE LITTLE MARE.

A peasant had a young son. The child's mother being about to die called him to her, and charged him solemnly to take good care of a little mare she owned, saying that by doing so he would be richly rewarded. The boy promised; his mother soon died, and in a very short time his father took another wife. His stepmother, not loving the boy, wickedly persuaded her husband to allow her to make away with him. One day she made for him some poisoned fritters. He had not lately given much care to his promise, but luckily he bethought himself of it that day, and the mare, after chiding him, told him how it was better late than never on account of his great danger. Thus warned he went home, where the stepmother fondled him more than usual; but, saying he was ill, he only ate a bit of dry bread. It happened the same with some cake that she cooked for him a few days after: unfortunately, however, this time the mare was overheard warning him. Resolving then to kill the mare also, she called her doctor, who wickedly consented to aid her. They agreed that she should feign illness, and that he should then advise, as the only cure, that she should wrap her body in the skin of a mare just killed. The mare, who knew everything, told the boy of it, and said that, to avoid suspicion, he was to advise killing her, but that, at midnight, he should come to the stable, whence they would escape together. So it was done, and after many days' travelling they arrived at a great city. "Now," said the mare, "I will put you in the way of making your fortune, but it will be necessary that, until I give you leave, you utter not a word excepting 'Bismé,' which shall serve as your name." She charged him also to hide always his beautiful golden hair by tying it up in a kerchief. She then sent him to the king's garden to seek work. The gardener took him, nor had reason to be sorry, for all that Bismé touched prospered beyond belief. In the garden stood the palace, where lived the king with his three daughters It was Bismé's duty to carry them flowers, above all on their feast-days, and they declared that they had never seen such fine ones. When came the saint's day of the youngest her flowers were the best of all, and she was much touched by their loveliness as well as by the beauty and modesty of Bismé, who seemed not even to dare to speak when addressed. The little mare now told him that he should go and dress his hair at midnight in a far corner of the garden, which, without his knowing it, was just under the princess's window. There he went, and untying the kerchief which bound his locks about his head, they fell in a golden shower over his shoulders. The princess, who had just come into her room, was dazzled by a strange brightness which lit it, and looking from the window to learn the cause she was startled to see that it was the golden hair of Bismé, who, all unconscious, was arranging it beneath her. The same thing happened on three nights, and the princess could no longer overcome the love for Bismé which had sprung up in her bosom. Her sisters had married princes of neighbouring countries, and a king had come to ask her hand of her father. In spite of her father's wishes, who told her she would never have another so fine an offer, she would not consent. Wondering at such strange behaviour, he asked her if she wanted to become a nun. For a long time she was sad and ailing, and the king, touched at the sight, offered to do anything to make her again happy. Having obtained his word, which kings may never break, she avowed her love for Bismé and her longing to marry him. "Be it so," said her father, "since I have given you my sacred word; but I can no longer treat you as my daughter; you must go with him to share the life of a poor gardener." She chose to follow the feelings of her heart, and became at once his wife and a peasant.

Very soon a war broke out, and her two brothers-in-law made ready to take part. A battle was about to be fought, and, in order to have as many men as possible, the king wished them to take Bismé. They mocked at him, asking what good such a lad could do; but they finally let him go. They gave him, however, such a wretched horse that he soon found himself fast in the mud of the road, whence his horse had not the strength to struggle out, and his brothers-in-law rode off laughing at him. No sooner were they out of sight than the little mare appeared beautifully harnessed, and with superb armour for Bismé, who, mounting her, quickly arrived on the field of battle. He there did wonders of bravery, and capturing more banners than he could carry he was forced to be content with the lances which surmounted them. He then rode home unrecognised, and having concealed his trophies put on again his poor garments. The enemy having been utterly defeated by his valour, the brothers-in-law gathered the banners he had left and carried them to the king as their own spoil. Then was set on foot a great banquet in honour of the victory, to find game for which the princes started for the chase. They took with them Bismé in the same scornful way, and soon he had the same ill-luck with his wretched hack. Again came up the little mare, bringing him a fine hunting dress with weapons, which he used with such success that he could scarcely carry all the game. Meeting without knowing him, the princes asked him to sell it. This he refused, but offered it them in exchange for their wedding rings. They accepted, resolving to buy others before returning, so that their wives should not know of it, and they carried the game home, pretending to have taken it themselves. The next day happened a similar adventure. Bismé was this time again beautifully equipped, though quite differently, and as before unrecognised. Now he demanded for his game that they should allow themselves to be branded with his seal on the rump. Strange to say they consented, believing it would never be known, and carried home the game with the same falsehood.

The day of the feast arrived. There was a throng of princes and knights, but among the servants stood Bismé and his poor wife, who was beginning to suffer sorely from grief and shame, in spite of her love for her husband. The two brothers-in-law bragged of their prowess in war and the chase, and showed proudly the banners, sneering the meanwhile at Bismé. The little mare at last gave him leave to speak, and he recounted all that had happened, showing as proof the lances and the wedding rings, and forcing his brothers-in-law to confess how he had branded them. The king, enraged at their perfidy, and struck by the virtues of Bismé, banished them for ever from his kingdom, and, taking in their stead Bismé and his wife, named him his heir.

THE GREAT BEAST.

A merchant, who had three daughters, being about to set forth on a long voyage, asked each of them what present she would like him to bring back for her. The eldest wished a bonnet, the second a gown, and the youngest only a rose. He went on his journey, and, his business done, he started on his way home. Passing one night through a wood he lost his way, and after wandering for a long while his horse became so jaded that he could go no further. Seeing a garden hard by he went near, and found the gate wide open, but he could find no living being. He entered, and beheld within a beautiful palace. Having put his horse in the stable, which seemed to have been made ready for him, he then turned his steps towards the palace. It was open and entirely deserted, though a bed was ready made, and a splendid dinner set out. He began to dine, and was deftly served by unseen hands. Immediately after eating, over-come by fatigue, he went at once to bed and soon fell soundly asleep until the morning, in spite of his uneasiness at his strange surround-ings. When he had arisen his breakfast was given him, and his horse cared for in the same mysterious way. The morning being fine, he started early on his journey, and he crossed the garden without seeing a soul, and marvelling greatly at what had befallen him. Just before reaching the gate his eye was caught by the sight of a rose of singular beauty. Recalling his daughter's wish, he picked it, when at once sprang up before him a dreadful monster, who, in great wrath threatened him with death for having stolen the loveliest and rarest ornament of his garden. "I never dreamt I was doing so much harm," said the frightened merchant, and he recounted to him the wish of his daughter. The beast seemed interested, asked many questions about her, and at last said that though he had been robbed of what was most dear to him he would pardon him if the daughter was given to him. "Begone," said he, "but return within three days or you shall all die." The father felt forced to promise, but when he reached home he had not the heart to tell her the wretched lot that awaited her. Seeing him always sad she questioned him, and ended by knowing all; and, as two days were already gone, and the palace far away, she unselfishly begged him to start at once. Hastening, with all speed, they reached the palace of the beast when but a few minutes were left of the third day, and found him in a pitiable state, half dead. They set to work to nurse him, and when he had rallied the merchant tore himself away from his daughter with sad forebodings. Two years passed, during which she lived in the palace, seeing the beast daily, when one day, after much urging, she besought the beast to give her leave to pay a short visit to her family, whom she had not since seen. " Remain but three days," said the beast, " or you will find me dead." She came back the third day, but by ill luck so late that she found the beast dying. So good had he been to her that she had become very fond of him, and she was overwhelmed with remorse at the evil she had unwillingly done him. She tended him lovingly, and, when he had come to himself, spoke tender words to him, promising never again to leave him, and even to become his wife. No sooner had she said this than the beast turned into a young and handsome prince; for it was this promise that he had to await. They were married at once, and ever after lived happily together.

JOHN OF CALAIS.

A merchant, who had gained much wealth in trading voyages to foreign parts, had an only son. When the boy became of age his father told him that he must work, so he loaded a ship with goods and entrusted it to him. He charged him to look well after his money, which the son promised and departed. He sailed to a far country, where he quickly sold all at great gain. Walking one day he came upon the rotting corpse of a man lying on the ground by the roadside. His flesh was being eaten by the crows, and no one would bury him. He was filled with horror and pity at the sight. Asking the passers-by why he was so left, he was told that it was the body of a bankrupt, who, having died without leaving wherewith to pay his debts, it was the law and custom to throw his body on the high road to be eaten up

by the crows. He then begged to know whether there was no way of
being allowed to bury him, for the young man had a good and tender
heart. This his father knowing was the reason why he had so charged
him to be careful lest he should part foolishly with his money. The
neighbours answered that the only way was to pay the debts, which
were very great. John at once agreed and paid all, so heavy a sum
that he had nothing left. Then, having given the body a decent burial,
he set sail and went home. His father on hearing of his coming made
ready a great feast, and soon after they met asked if he had made a
good sale. Yes, said the son, and he told him all. He was not at all
pleased with what he thought the wastefulness of his son, but he ended
by forgiving him this time. After a while he sent him on a second
voyage, now charging him sternly to be more careful, and for greater
safety he told the captain not to let him go on shore alone. He gave
him still more precious goods, which the son took to another far city,
and gained still greater profit than before. To make sure not to go back
again with empty hands he at once set sail for home. He was almost
there when he met a Moorish pirate ship, in which were two captive
women, one of them young and very beautiful. His kind heart gave
way, and wishing to ransom them they would take no less than their
weight in gold. John of Calais at once paid it, though it left him
without a penny. Having brought them on his ship he asked them
their names. "I cannot tell you mine," said the younger, "but my
companion is named Isabel, and she is my governess." The ship soon
reached home and he was met with a loving welcome until his father
learned that he brought back nothing but two women. He flew into
a great rage, saying, "You have nearly ruined me, and I will do no
more for you but give you a cottage, a small bit of land, and a thousand francs ; manage as you can ; I wish never to see you again."

John took to his new home the two women, and at once married the
younger. He worked hard, and after a while laid up enough money
to buy a small ship, with which he made short voyages. His wife
showed herself well brought up and skilful in every way. She was a
good artist, and one day she gave him a life-like portrait in silk of
herself, him, and their child, which she bade him fasten before the

prow of his ship. He was then making ready for a voyage to Portugal, and without saying why she told him he was to drag his ship on shore by the prow.* Having arrived, he did so, and he was soon surprised to see a crowd about his ship. They looked keenly at the picture, and said to one another, "It is she; certainly she." An officer of the court came up and asked him to follow him. They went together, and John to his great astonishment was brought before the king. He was asked who were the persons in the picture, and was made to tell how he had found his wife, for it seemed she was the daughter of the king, who had had no tidings of her since she was captured. The king, overjoyed that she was still alive, got ready a fleet of ships to bring her home, and bade John lead the ships to his town. In them went many lords and ladies of the court, among whom one who was betrothed to the princess when she was made prisoner. John's father, hearing of the fleet's coming and all that had happened, was alarmed, and hurried to bring from her cottage the princess and governess, hoping to hide from the king their hard treatment. The princess at once set sail for home, and on the voyage she soon saw that her old lover still hoped to marry her after putting her husband out of the way by foul play. He tried to talk to her of love, but she drove him away, forbidding him to come near her. He then began to plot against John. The princess, mistrusting him, besought her husband never to leave her on the voyage, urged him to let himself be tied to her by the leg with a little golden chain. But one day he heard them cry that a great fish was to be seen, and they begged him as a skilful fisher to come and help catch it. He ran eagerly, without thinking, and in the bustle a way was found to make him fall overboard as if by chance. The ship went on without trying to save him, for the princess knew nothing until too late. Happily for him, a little boat came by, and the man in it took him in. They landed on a wretched desert island, where they barely lived on the fish they caught. But they shared everything fairly, and lived there together a long time. John was sad with such a life, but his companion gave him no hope of a change. However, at last he said

* This is done at many ports on the Riviera.

that he would take him to his family if he would bind himself to give him the half of what he held most dear whenever he should ask him. John did so, and soon found himself in Portugal. He had greatly changed, his body wasted, his beard overgrown, and his clothes in rags, so that few would know him. One day, being in a city which seemed strange to him, he came to a palace where a feast was being made ready. Men were going up and down the staircase, laden with wood and water. Said he to himself, "Perhaps I may do the same, and thus gain something to eat." Soon he was asked to help, and he went to work. While passing through an ante-room he met a lady, who looked sharply at him, and followed him. After having well studied him she said to herself, "I am sure it is he," and ran to tell her mistress the news. For he had come into the king's palace unawares, having been there but once before, and that only for a moment, and this lady was the governess. The princess had him brought to her rooms, where with the greatest joy they at once knew one another. It was, however, needful awhile to hide him. Unluckily, this feast was on account of her wedding, for all believed her husband drowned, and after waiting a suitable time the king wished her to wed again in spite of her unhappiness at the thought. Hoping still that John was alive, and yet feeling helpless against her father's will, she sought to gain time, and succeeded in putting off the wedding for a year and a day. This had passed, and her betrothed claimed her hand. Now she feigned to be ill in order to delay, while she and the governess bettered John's sad state so that he would be known. From him she first learned how he had been the victim of a shameful crime, and she now set her heart on punishing the wretch as he deserved. She at last hit upon a plan. To avoid mistrust she allowed the wedding to be made ready. The king had commanded a show of fireworks, and this gave her the chance she sought. She asked her betrothed from love of her to light one piece, which had been privately so made that he was hurled into the air as if by chance, and so ended his days. Soon John's return was made known, and the king, having been told of all, welcomed him as his son, causing the feast to be given in his honour. All were making merry, the princess and he were in a heaven of joy, when a mysterious stranger appeared. Asking to speak with John on pressing business, the servants at first refused to let him in at such a time, but he urged so hard that John, being told, agreed to see him.   Having been brought into the room where all the family were, he found that it was the man who had saved his life when he was thrown into the sea, and who had now come to claim the fulfilment of his hard bargain.   His dismay was dreadful, but being a man of his word he at once showed him his son as his dearest possession, and drawing his sword was about to cut him in twain when the unknown staid his hand, saying, " I loose you from your vow, for I am he whose body you piously buried when it had been thrown on the high road, and was being picked to pieces by the crows."

J. B. ANDREWS.

ANANCI STORIES.

THESE stories come from Mr. W. A. B. Musgrave, of Balliol College, the son of Sir Anthony Musgrave, Governor of Jamaica. They were told him by his nurse, a Mulatto woman, born in Antigua, who, when asked who Ananci was, said he was the spider.

I.

Ananci went out for a walk one day, and as he was passing through a wood he came to an open space in which a table was laid out for a large number of guests. Ananci, always greedy, looked around him, and seeing no sign of any one fell to and ate up the whole of it. This dinner had been prepared for the animals, who had not to wait long for an opportunity of punishing Ananci, for he on his return home found his wife storing yams. Being very fond of them he asked her for some, but she refused to give them unless he could tell her the true name of a yam. "I know," said Ananci, "Yam name a Coosh-acoosh, a Redinyam." "No," said his wife, "You no right: you mus' go off to you mother and she will tell you what yam real name." So off went Ananci to his mother's house. When he got there he burst in and asked, "Mother, what yam real name?" "A Nyam-pinya," said his mother. As soon as he heard this, away he went for home, and for fear of forgetting the name he kept on repeating it and humming to himself "Oo-oo-oooo Nyampinya, oo-oo-oooo Nyampinya." Now it so happened that he had to pass through the same wood which he had gone through in the morning, and in which he had eaten the dinner. And when he had reached the spot where the table had been he was met by the ox who greeted him with "Good-day bra 'Nanci," "Good-day bra ox, oo-oo-oooo Nyam——" "Eh! stop, bra 'Nanci.

What yam name?" As soon as he was asked this question Ananci forgot all about the name he had been told and answered "A Cooshacoosh, a Redinyam." And he went on his way humming "Oo-oo-oooo Cooshacoosh, oo-oo-oooo Redinyam," till he got home. "Well 'Nanci," said his wife, "what yam name?" "A Cooshacoosh, a Redinyam." "No," says she, "you mus' go back." So off he went again, and on his way back met the horse. The scene with the ox was repeated, and he was again sent away by his wife. Next time he met the mule, and so on, till all the animals that were to have been at the dinner had stopped him and had asked him the same question. At last he managed to reach home, singing "Oo-oo-oooo Nyampinya:" but by that time there was only one yam left unstored, and that was all he could get.

II.

Ananci having been taken by his enemies, it was determined to get rid of him by throwing him into the sea. So he was tied up in a sack and given to two men who were to take him down to the sea-shore and drown him. As he was carried along he sang "Me too nyung, me too nyung, me too nyung, me too nyung, me too nyung to marry king's darter." The men were much amused and said "Oh! you goin' to marry king's darter are you? Come along." But as Ananci was heavy and the day was hot they went into a house they came to to get a drink, and left the sack outside with Ananci singing his song in it. And while they were in the house a young fellow came along the road with a flock of sheep. When he heard Ananci's song he said "Eh bra! you goin' to marry king's darter?" "Oh yes, bra," answered Ananci, "but me too nyung to do it." "Me ole 'nuff," said the other, and offered to change places with Ananci. So Ananci made him untie the sack, and got out. Then he put the young fellow into it, tied him up, and went off with the flock of sheep. By-and-bye the men came out, picked up the sack, and went on towards the sea. And as they went the young fellow inside sang "Me ole 'nuff, me ole 'nuff, me ole 'nuff, me ole 'nuff, me ole 'nuff to marry king's darter." "Oh!" said the men, "you ole 'nuff now are you?" and laughed. When they got to the sea they took a boat and rowed out a long way.

When they thought they were far enough from the shore they dropped the sack overboard and rowed back. Ananci meanwhile had driven his sheep down to the sea to meet them on their return. So that the first thing they saw when they landed was, to their astonishment, Ananci himself with his flock. "Eh! bra 'Nanci," said they, "you come back from under the sea?" "Oh yes, bra," said Ananci, "and I brought all dese along wid me. Plenty more down dere where dese come from."

J. B. ANDREWS.

PROVERBS: ENGLISH AND KELTIC,

WITH THEIR EASTERN RELATIONS.

[Read at the Meeting of the Society on Tuesday, 13 April, 1886, and circulated in proof among the Members. It is now printed as a tentative introduction to the subject.]

Y duties in India for 30 years in connection with popular education and oriental literature led me into close connection with the masses and consequently with their Folk-Lore and their Proverbs which represent the wit and wisdom of the multitude, while the preparation in England of a work illustrating the Bible from Emblems and Oriental Proverbs has drawn me on the track of the present Essay.

THE USE OF PROVERBS IN REFERENCE TO THE PEOPLE, GEOGRAPHY, FEMALES, PHILOLOGY.

In these days of travelling and of judging a people by outside showy appearances it is well to remember that " Proverbs are the unwritten but fondly treasured literature of a people from which some insight into the thoughts and opinions which govern their actions may be gained." The proper study of mankind is man. How, for instance, that Chinese proverb expresses the narrow national feeling,

> A girl is worth one-tenth of a boy's worth.
> When there is no fish in the river shrimps are valued.

How to improve the common people is the question of the day; but to do this efficiently we must know them, while their proverbs would soon teach us by the amount of acuteness and observation they evince not to despise them but rather to admire their feelings. You will find among the common people few book-learned, but you will see many who have read God's great book of nature in a way that would put to shame many scholars; the literary tribe and the penmen may despise them as clodhoppers, but they know little of their proverbs, which are crystallisations of wit and wisdom; the learned have known books better than men, hence much of the neglect by the literary world of proverbs, "*odi vulgus et arceo.*"

Coins have occupied the attention of the learned and have yielded valuable knowledge of kings and of the upper strata of society; proverbs, coins of wisdom, bear the stamp of the millions.

In geographical and historical science much aid may be obtained by tracing out the references to places and to historical characters given in proverbs. Isaac Taylor, in his valuable work on *Words and Places*, states that nearly all the river names in England are Keltic, and many of these names and places are enshrined in proverbs. The Arabic proverbs are distinguished by the constant references to persons, things, and places; the Anglo-Keltic must have them to a certain degree, but little has been done in this way of exploration.

Proverbs are, as Professor Wilson observes, valuable accessories to the correct delineation of national manners and opinions, or as Tennyson defines them,

> Jewels five words long
> That, on the stretched forefingers of all time,
> Sparkle for ever.

They throw light on the condition of the country. Dr. Johnson made severe remarks on the treeless condition of Scotland; but ages before an English proverb expressed the same view, " Had Judas betrayed Christ in Scotland he might have repented before he could have found a tree to hang himself on."

The females of India are fond of playing at proverbs; but even in England, as recent as the days of Lord Bacon, what was called crossing proverbs, proverb play, battles of proverbs, were favourite games at court. Queen Elizabeth was very fond of them, they were played by one person producing a proverb, which the opponent immediately brought another to contradict. D'Israeli, in his *Curiosities of Literature*, gives an example of the game:—

Proverb. The world is a long journey.
Opposite. Not so: the sun goes it every day.

Proverb. It is a great way to the bottom of the sea.
Opposite. Not so: it is but a stone's cast.

Proverb. The pride of the rich makes the labour of the poor.
Opposite. Not so: the labours of the poor make the pride of the rich.

The best proverbs are found among women. In collecting proverbs in Bengal I employed women to go amongst their own sex for this purpose, and I can fully confirm the truth of Dr. Phalloon's statement in his Hindustani Dictionary. " In the speech of the women of India is mirrored the very image of the thoughts and feelings by which humanity is moved by the burning words which are wrung from the sharper sufferings of the weaker vessel. The songs composed by the women are distinguished by a natural charm and yet simple pathos, which make their way to the heart. The seclusion of the women in India has been the asylum of the true vernacular, as pure and simple as it is unaffected by the pedantry of word-makers. Many of the most caustic and terse epigrams of the language have their birth in these isolated women's apartments, whose inmates are jealously barred from any communication with strange men."

Proverbs are often nuts difficult to crack, referring to local customs, &c. &c.; thus the Afghans say " Wealth is a Hindu's beard." I never met an Englishman who saw the force of it, and yet it is simply explained by the practice of the Hindus: as they have many relations they are obliged to shave often as a sign of mourning. The proverb is equivalent to the Scripture saying, "Riches fly away as an eagle to heaven." Proverbs are designed to exercise the ingenuity, like the Modern Greek proverb, "Eggs but not wings," *i. e.* mere promises but no performance.

One important bearing of proverbs on Folk-Lore is the light they throw on the people in their inmost thoughts and on the recesses of social life. In philology they serve as a guide to the genuine meaning of words—this has been practically tested by two important works recently published—one in Russia, the other in India. We refer to the Russian Dictionary of Dahl and the Hindustani Dictionary of Dr. Phalloon. Very different from Dr. Johnson, who illustrates his dictionary by quotations from books only, they go to the living voice of the people as given in their proverbs—to the rustic mother-tongue, the unadulterated language of women, the every-day speech of the people, depicted in their songs, poetry, and proverbs; the examples quoted give an insight into the domestic and social life of the people, their morals, religious beliefs, the inmost thoughts of the inner life of the people, expressed in a racy language, not the stilted language of Pandits and pedants. Sir J. Davis says on this point, "Chinese proverbs are of great value as illustrating every law of the language."

English Proverbs, to be compared with foreign ones, especially with Eastern.

Large collections of English Proverbs have been made, as the works of Camden, Howell, Ray, Bohn, and a host of others point out,* but they are deficient in classification, and the compilers seem never to have entertained the idea of comparing them with the proverbs of Eastern or Slav nations, and thereby gaining a clue to their origin and affinities. It is only now however that this can be ·done satisfactorily, owing to the light thrown by comparative philology and to the researches made into Eastern lore. As the English language is best studied by the light thrown on it by comparative philology, and as a knowledge of human anatomy is greatly aided by the discoveries in the comparative anatomy of animals, so must English Proverbiology be assisted by the light reflected from comparative Proverbiology.†

Comparing ourselves with ourselves is not only unwise in moral but also in intellectual subjects; it narrows the view; you become what the Hindus call *munduk kup*, a frog in a well, the oriental expression for cockneyism. England is an empire on which the sun never sets, hence insular notions do not become her; we must rise from *Great* Britain to the dignity of the *Greater* Britain. England is an island, and

* *Proverbial Folk-Lore*, by the Rev. A. Cheales, Vicar of Brockham, Surrey, is a work of singular merit in its interesting classification and illustrations by proverbs.

† Kelly's *Proverbs of all Nations compared, explained, and illustrated*, is a good work, but his "*all* Nations" excludes Russian, Indian, Slav, Chinese, most important factors; the work is, however, of value, showing the light the proverbs of one nation reflect on the other, and the *unitas in diversitate* among them. Masson, in St. Petersburg, has produced a work on a similar plan, comparing chiefly Russian, German, Italian, Spanish, Slav, and English proverbs.

therefore has insular tendencies, but science has made the ocean a con-
necting link and not a line of separation; India for instance by sea is
more accessible to London than Siberia is by land to St. Petersburg.
Let this Society then, having its seat in a cosmopolitan city, rise to the
dignity of its situation by viewing English Folk-Lore in its affinities
with that of other nations and especially with Eastern ones. Few people
are cognisant of the fact that the Brahman of Benares, the Priest of
Moscow, and the Dean of Westminster speak a language radically the
same, and mutually understood by their common ancestry when they
lived together 3,000 years ago on the plains of Central Asia, their
primitive residence.

KELTIC PROVERBS AND THE ENGLISH RACE, NOT ANGLO-SAXON.

Though the Keltic wave has now receded to the West of Europe,
submerged by the Saxon as the Slav of Central Europe was by the
Teutonic, yet it has left deep historical traces, " footprints on the sands
of time." Isaac Taylor, in his excellent work on *Words and Places*,
shows that the names of rivers and countries in Europe enable us to
trace the wide diffusion of the Keltic race and to follow their progress
across Europe. "Cymraic roots are found scattered over Spain, North
Italy, Switzerland, and South Germany, countries which were occupied
by the Kelts." There is a strong resemblance between the Kelts and
ancient Greeks in their emotional and oratorical powers: the two races
were connected in former days, while Druidism and the Greek
philosophy had much in common. The Keltic proverbs are therefore
worth comparing with the Greek and the Slav.

It is important to trace out the Keltic element in English proverbs,—
which ought to be found,—for the popular idea that the ancient Britons,
a Keltic race, were driven by the Saxons from central and north England
to the mountains of Wales is now fading away before the light of facts.*
The term Anglo-Saxon race is therefore now an inappropriate one,

---

* See several excellent articles on this subject by the Rev. J. Davies in the
Archæologia Cambrensis, in which he shows, from historical and philological
sources, that the English people is formed to a considerable extent from Keltic
elements neither exterminated nor absorbed by the conquerors, who intermarried

for Kelt, Dane, and Roman contributed as much as Saxon to build up the present imperial race, and the *élan* exhibited by the English in their Colonial and Indian Empire could never have been communicated by the solid but slow Saxon; the phlegmatic Saxon differed too widely in temperament from the emotional Kelt or fiery Welshman to suppose that the English are of pure Teutonic origin; the English stand out distinct from either the Saxon or the Kelt; partaking of the many characteristics of each, they unite the impetuosity and enterprise of the Kelt with the solid persevering temper of the Saxon. The English Kelts, however, got from the Saxons and Danes an infusion of Hyperborean blood which improved their nautical skill, while the Normans, of Scandinavian descent, polished their rudeness by the refinements of chivalry. An American therefore justly remarks, that this mixed race of English is no more Anglo-Saxon than it is Roman-Phœnician—a great blessing, as amalgams are good in chemistry and equally so with races. The English race like its language is an amalgam. How often the remark is made of an old race that it is deteriorating from want of the infusion of new blood.*

WELSH PROVERBS, THEIR ANTIQUITY. HOWEL. THE BASQUES.

The proverbial Folk-Lore of the Welsh or Ancient Britons is very valuable in itself and also in serving as a clue to our connections with the East, though, according to Skene, there was an Iberian or Basque people, a long-headed, dark-skinned Asiatic race, which preceded the Kelts in England. An extraordinary theory is propounded by Wilson and others, that the Ancient Britons as well as the Saxons are of Israelitish

---

with the Kelts and cultivated the land by their aid, for, as Sir F. Palgrave also thinks, a large British or Keltic element must have remained on the soil. The Saxons, coming over in small ships and without wives, could have been too few to cultivate the land. History shows that the Loegrians, or natives of England from the Thames to the Humber, coalesced with the Saxons, and finally were blended with them. The Cambrians or Welsh did not so coalesce, though they retained for a time many places in the South of England.

* Aubrey's "Remains of Gentilisme and Judaisme" ought to throw some light on the ancient Kelt.

origin—"Israel's grave was the Saxon's birthplace." One thing may
be admitted in this, the Ten Tribes and the ancestors of the English
once lived together in Central Asia ere the Exodus took place towards
the setting sun. Did the Ten Tribes emigrate about the same period?
Are the Jews in the Krimea a remnant of them? We should inquire
whether any old proverbs throw light on this.

Howel, historiographer to Charles the Second, who has written in his
"Paræmiologia" a most valuable book on proverbs, states regarding
the antiquity of Welsh proverbs: "The Cambrian proverbs were
frequent among the Bards; some of them reached to the Druids, from
whom they received their first rise long ere the Roman eagles planted
their talons on the island." He has given in his work more than 2,000
Welsh proverbs with an English translation. A new edition of these,
with notes and classified, might serve as a basis for a work on Welsh
proverbs.

CORNWALL, FIRST SPANISH THEN KELTIC—ITS PROVERBS.

Skene in his *Celtic Scotland* gives various reasons in favour of
the view "that the population of the Scilly Isles, Cornwall, and South
Wales, was Iberian; an examination of the ancient sepulchral remains in
Britain gives us reason to suppose that a people possessing these physical
characteristics had once spread over the whole of both of the British
Isles." Dr. Thurnam concludes from the examination of skulls that
"Britain was inhabited in the neolithic age by a long-headed people,
and that towards its close it was invaded by a bronze-using race, who
were dominant during the bronze age. This Iberian or Basque population spread over the whole of Britain and Ireland, inhabiting caves,
and burying their dead in caves and chambered tombs just as in the
Iberian peninsula also in the neolithic age." See Dawkins's *Care
Hunting*. These Basques or Biscayans were ancient Spaniards, who,
like the Welsh, lived in the mountains away from the Roman conquerors. Huxley, in his *Critiques and Addresses*, p. 167, maintains
that an Iberian or Basque people preceded the Kelts in Great Britain
or Ireland; they settled in Cornwall as tin merchants, the Scilly Isles

being their entrepôt.   Greek and Roman historians refer to this dark race.   Oikenhart published in 1847 an edition of 537 Basque proverbs with a preface by Michel, which may be of use on the question.

Cornwall, that wild but mysterious land, styled by the Greeks an island, teems with interest for Folk-Lore people ; it may have been originally colonised to a limited extent from Spain and from Phœnicia; few of the Keltic race now remain, for some of its people, along with the South Bretons, left at the time of the early Saxon wars and emigrated to Bretagne, whose language is similar.   Still a strong leaven must have remained in Cornwall and in the South of England, for, in the time of Alfred, Somerset and Wilts were Keltic, and Athelstan found the Saxons and Kelts in joint possession of Exeter, until he drove out the latter.   Down to the reign of Henry the Eighth Keltic was the language of Cornwall.   About one-tenth of the proper names in Cornwall are of Keltic origin.   See Sauvé's *Breton Proverbs*, Campion, Paris, 1878.   We want a similar work on Cornish proverbs, but classified and annotated.

MANX PROVERBS, A DESIDERATUM.

The Isle of Man or Mona, inhabited successively by Britons, Scots or Picts, and Norwegians, is an interesting field for Proverbs.   In the " Transactions of the Manx Society," vol. 21, there is a collection of Manx proverbs, and an interesting essay has been published by the Rev. T. Wilson on Manx Proverbs.*

THE GYPSIES' PROVERBS, ORIENTAL, WITH A MIXTURE OF GREEK AND SLAV.

That singular race the Gypsies, "tribes of the weary feet and wandering eye," deserve our attention ; they are Nats or Sudras of India, who, impelled by their roving habits and love of plunder, fled from the ruthless persecution of Timor about 1408, when he put 500,000 Hindus to the sword for not becoming Musulmans.   They came probably by the Persian Gulf through the deserts of Arabia to Egypt, which gave them

* They curiously correspond with the Irish : *e.g.* Manx—Bio chabbyl as yiow bee; *Irish*—Live horse and you'll get grass.

their name. In France they appeared about 1427. In Henry the Eighth's time a fine of 40*l.* was imposed on any one that imported a Gypsy; and still there are 16,000 in England and about 750,000 in all Europe.

Their language is not the slang or cant of thieves, but has Hindustani as the basis mixed with Slavonic and Modern Greek. I have heard it spoken on the banks of the Volga, in Servia, Moscow, the Alhambra, Seville.* Their proverbs must be of philological value. The Gypsies sometimes eat carrion, justifying the practice by the proverb, "That which God kills is better than that which man kills." They are not fond of sheep, quoting the proverb, "Despise those who risk their neck for their bellies." The Spanish Gypsies recommend a deceiving tongue by the following, "The poor fool who closeth his mouth never winneth a dollar," "The river which runneth with sound bears along with it stones and water."

Though there are 150 books on the Gypsies we have no English work on the Gypsies equalling in interest Pouskin's Russian poem on the Tsigani describing the life and feeling of the Gypsies. The following are a few of the Russian proverbs on the Gypsies:

" A Gypsy once in his life tells the truth but then he repents of so doing."

" A Gypsy cannot live a single day without cheating."

" Where a Jew could not go the Gypsy crept."

The modern Greeks have a proverb on the Gypsies, "Go to the Gypsy children and choose the whitest," *i. e.* when all is bad whatever you choose must be equally bad. Barrow, in his *Gypsies in Spain,* speaks of the Gypsy language as "in all principal points one and the same, though more or less corrupted by foreign words. One remarkable feature must not be passed over without notice, namely, the very considerable number of Slavonic words which are to be found embedded in it, whether it be spoken in Spain or Germany, in England or Italy: from which circumstance we are led to the conclusion that these people,

---

* The following are some of the common words which are Indian: *Dures,* day; *Ratte,* night; *Baro,* great; *Kalo,* black; *Rup,* silver; *Bal,* hair; *Aok,* eye; *Kan,* ear; *Mui,* mouth; *Dant,* teeth; *Raja,* king; *Gree,* horse; *Kar,* house; *Pani,* water; *Barapane,* ocean; *Dad,* father; *Mutchi,* fish.

in their way from the East, travelled in one large compact body, and that their route lay through some region where the Sclavonian language or a dialect thereof was spoken." He supposes that to have been Bulgaria, where they tarried a considerable period as nomadic herdsmen, and where numbers are at the present day: "There are even a greater quantity of terms of modern Greek, a language which they used for centuries and learned in Roumania: there is more of modern Persian in their language than of either the Greek or Slav."

Insular Egotism.

We are happily waking up more and more from our insular egotism and feeling the responsibilities of empire which connects us by literary, political, social, religious, and commercial ties with the East, the regions whence our ancestors came and brought not only religious traditions and customs with them, but also Folk-Lore. Were not proverbs brought also?—those gems which express the people's thoughts, and which survive the wreck of empires and the change of dynasties.

The Affinity of Anglo-Keltic with Eastern Proverbs.

The works of Pictet (Origines Indo-Européennes), Eichhof, Bopp, prove fully the affinity of the Keltic with the Indian languages, and that the Welsh, the Brahmin, and the Russian, spoke languages radically the same. A very excellent pamphlet on this subject has just appeared, "The Keltic Languages in relation to other Tongues," by the Rev. J. Davies, a gentleman who like Whitley Stokes combines two qualifications which are rare in these days, being both a ripe Sanskrit as well as Keltic scholar. He shows in his book that many words claimed to be of Latin or German origin are pure Keltic.

Ralston has pointed out the affinity of the Folk-Tales of Europe with those of Asia, stating they are heirlooms of the Aryan family, developed by various branches of the family from mythological germs, which existed in the minds of our primeval ancestors while they still inhabited their ancient homes in the highlands of Central Asia. Many instances might be brought forward of stories now current in different parts of Europe as folk-tales preserved by early tradition, which were centuries ago written down in Asia and embedded in books. With these affinities then in language and Folk-Lore, proverbs claim a special place; they well up from the depths of the human heart and travel like the dog with man; they represent the wit and wisdom of the multitude as handed down through a long series of generations ; " when kings and dynasties toppled over, these stood erect amid the billows of time." Languages become modernised, but old proverbs are a species of fossil-poetry, and of these it may be said, as Tennyson wrote of the brook—

> For men may come and men may go,
> But I go on for ever.

As the ancient Britons spoke Keltic, surely there must be traces of it in the old English proverbs,* which like proverbs generally photograph social life, and contain a treasury of archaic words with constant reference to Folk-Lore, geographical and historical names.

Prince Louis Bonaparte has done nobly in publishing specimens of the dialects of England. We ought to have a book on the dialectical differences of English proverbs.

The story of Whittington and his cat was known several centuries ago in Persia, and probably existed at a much earlier period in India and also in Russia. Benfey ascribes to the Mongols, in consequence of their long ascendancy over so large a part of the east of Europe, a great influence over European popular fiction, and maintains that India was the source from whence the folk-tales of the present day streamed forth, originally disseminated by the Buddhist people and further transmitted by the Mahommedans.

Now as many proverbs are offshoots of tales, parables, &c. have we not a clue to guide us? Is it then to be supposed that with affinity between the Anglo-Kelts and the East in language, folk-lore, and institutions, there is none in proverbs, those fragments of ancient wisdom which, like oral tradition, stand the test of time.

---

* I have met one English proverb containing the Keltic word *capples* " 'Tis time to yoke when the cart comes to the capples (horses)."

THE VILLAGE SYSTEM OF INDIA, RUSSIA, ENGLAND.

We have an analogy with the East in the village system of Russia, which was common to England, Russia, and India. Mr. Gomme, our Secretary, in the Prospectus of his *Primitive Folkmoots* states : " All authorities agree that the germ of English institutions is to be traced from a primitive origin, but they do not seek to trace it by the evidences of British archæology alone. By adopting the new and more historical method, however, it is clearly shown that not only is there no necessity for appealing to Latin or early German history for much of the evidence of the early history of English institutions, but that it is possible to go further back into the archaic life of Britain than has yet been done." Sir H. Maine on Village Communities and Laveleye Sur le Propriété have both treated fully on this subject. Professor Sokalsko published in 1872 *Selskay Obtzina*, showing that the old village system in the Saxon times of England was like the old Russian village system. The village community was styled in Russ the *mir* or world. I give a few Russian proverbs referring to it :

" What the *mir* has arranged is God's decision." Cf. " Vox populi, vox Dei."

" Over the *mir* there is no judge but God."

" The *mir's* shoulder is broad, it will carry all."

" The *mir* sighs and the rock is rent asunder."

" A thread of the *mir* becomes a shirt for the naked."

The same institution existed in India, and with reference to the village jury or *panchayat* of five or ten * persons there are the following Bengali proverbs :

" If ten persons are gathered together, God is in the midst of them."

" I will go where ten go."

" Ten flowers together will make a nosegay."

CHINA THE LAND OF PROVERBS.

Asia is the land of proverbs; and among the countries most fruitful in them rank India and China; as to which is the richer we have no

* It is curious that, according to the early policy of the Anglo-Saxons, each village was divided into ten wards or petty districts; hence they are called tythings or decenniars, as the elder was denominated decennus or tything-man.

materials for coming to an accurate decision: but proverbs are extensively used in conversation in China. No matter what may be the topic, a proverb suitable to the occasion is very likely to be forthcoming, and any educated Chinese can write off long lists of proverbs from memory, while a great number are found in native books. On New Year's day a skilful penman writes out a number of proverbs on long strips of diverse colours; these are hung on door-posts, the pillars of houses, the masts of ships, &c. They are used in conversation to give it piquancy and flavour; many are cast in the form of parallelisms or couplets.

Parallel and Stray Proverbs.

The Aryan race, in their exodus from the plains of Central Asia to Europe, are considered to have taken two routes, one through Kherson and north of the Black Sea, the other from Armenia across the Caucasus to North Greece, thence by the Danube through Germany to England, which was also entered through Spain and Phœnicia; the latter country has left its memorial in England in the well-worship.

There was more travelling in former days than people fancy; the Northmen in the tenth century sailed to New England and settled colonies on that coast, and they are said to have been preceded in their voyage to Iceland and America by the Irish and Basques of Spain. The latter were adventurous fishermen and extensively engaged in the whale fishery; they were accustomed to visit the north-east coast of America long before the time of Columbus. The Phœnicians helped to colonise Ireland. Of certain Indian tribes of America it is said by Catlin they are the descendants of Welsh who left their land previous to its being subjugated by Edward the First, and who retained a number of pure Welsh words in their language. When in America in 1873 I made a search for Indian proverbs, but could get none.

The Gipsies, the last emigrants from India, travelled by the Euphrates Valley route, and arrived in Constantinople in the beginning of the fifteenth century; the main portion, then some 200,000, settled in Wallachia, and from thence they began to diverge. They arrived in Scotland about 1514. They number now about 750,000, of which Russia has 48,000, Spain 40,000, Hungary 159,000, Roumania 250,000;

there are in England about 16,000, of whom 2,000 are on the outskirts of London; they do not however retain the Hindu love of washing, but are fond of the pipe; "they will quarrel like Kilkenny cats over a penny, but they will kiss each other over the pipe."

Southern Russia and the Slavonic countries lying in the gangway of the route of emigration from Asia to Europe, their proverbs as a missing link are deserving of study; while the Kelts pushed on towards the sunset lands, the Slavs remained behind in the Danubian valley and Central Europe. Snegiref's work on Russian proverbs ought to be analysed in this respect, as well as Masson's "Mudrost Narodnaya," which compares Russian proverbs with German, French, Italian, English, Spanish; as also Dahl's "great Storehouse of 25,000 Russian Proverbs."

Proverbs, like certain geological strata, crop up in two countries wide apart without appearing in the intervening ones.

The word "commons," which signifies little to an Englishman, expresses an idea that has strayed from the East, viz. the village system, under which lands were held in common or by the community, as exists to this day in Russia, and has until lately been general in India. A similar term we have in Boxing Day, at Christmas; it is a corruption of *bukshis*, or presents, a word well known from Cairo to Calcutta.

EXAMPLES OF PARALLEL OR STRAY PROVERBS.

Proverbs are wandering sheep, and often stray far from their native place; so is it with many of the English proverbs, and so is it with the English alphabet, which has passed from the hands of the Phœnicians to the Greeks, then to the Italians, and was transmitted with various modifications to England. Of course there are many proverbs which have not strayed, but are the children of the soil, originating from the identity of human nature, and from what is common in feelings and wants to all men. Such are those on women, mothers-in-law, though they generally have a local colouring.

We shall give some illustrations. The English proverb, "a pig in a poke," equivalent to the Welsh "never buy a cat in a bag," has wandered from Greece, but, as is usual in straying proverbs, in a somewhat different garb and signification.   During Moslem ascendancy in Greece the people were not allowed to sell the pig, as it was an unclean animal, hence it was offered for sale in the night season hidden in a bag.   In Russia I often asked the meaning of the proverb, "Do not buy a priest's horse nor marry a widow's daughter."   The Russians did not clearly understand the reference to the widow's daughter; it seemed to them only to imply, have nothing to do with anything connected with the widow; but Ray in his English proverbs gives one having the meaning definitely, "He that marries a widow with three daughters marries four thieves."   The Spaniards have the same proverb.

The Turks say, "Of ten men nine are women."   A sharp satire both on men and women.   On which is it most severe?   I recently found the corresponding idea in an Afghan poet, Ashraf Khan.

> Since I, the separated, became acquainted with its secrets,
> I find the world hath countless women, but few, few men.

The Russians say, "Where the Turk's horse treads the grass grows not."   The same occurs in Ray's English Proverbs.   The Chinese say, "Where he's trodden no grass will grow."

"The nearer the church the further from God," runs through Germany, France, Italy, Holland.   In Welsh it is, "The nearer the church porch the further from Paradise."   But this is probably a mere loan.

The Russians impress the idea of the evils of society beginning in the upper classes by the proverb, "From the head the fish begins to stink."   The modern Greeks have the same.

The English " Walls have ears " occurs in Arabic and Tamul, and also in the Talmud.

"If you wish to learn to pray go to sea" is found in the Basque and Spanish.   In Polish it is, "He does not understand how to pray, he learns it when he goes to sea."   In Russian, "When you walk, pray once; when you go to sea, pray twice; when you go to be married, pray three times."

Arabic. " When the hen crows after the manner of a cock she should be killed."   *Russian.* "If you are a cock, crow; if a hen, lay eggs."   *Italian.* "It is a sad house where the hen crows louder than the cock."   *Scotch* and *Spanish* similar to the *Italian.*   The English speak of a *hen*-pecked husband.

Russian. "A Russian can be cheated only by a Gipsy, a Gipsy by a Jew, a Jew by a Greek, and a Greek by the devil."

Arabic. "Take a piece of mud, strike it against the wall, if it do not stick it will leave a mark," *i. e.* the effects of slander. Similar in English.

English. "There is a devil in every berry of the grape." Strayed from Turkey.

English. "A lie stands upon one leg, but truth upon two," a Jewish proverb also.

Russian. "My skin is nearer to me than my shirt." *Basque.* "The shirt touches me, but the skin is nearer to me, for it belongs to me." *English.* "Near is my shirt, but nearer is my skin," equivalent to "Charity begins at home."

Persian. "The worst day for the cock is when his feet are washed," *i. e.* before killing him. *Basque.* "The cock's feet are washed to his misfortune." *Bengali.* "The ant gets wings to his destruction," *i. e.* the crows then devour him. *Spanish.* "God gives the ant wings that she may perish the sooner."

English. "The kettle calling the pot black." *Basque.* "The crow reproached the young jackdaw for its black head." *Bengali.* "The sieve says to the needle you have a hole in your tail." *Bible.* "Why beholdest thou the mote in thy brother's eye, whilst a beam is in thine own."

Spanish. "Three women and one goose make a market."

English.	ditto	ditto
Italian.	ditto	three geese.

Polish. "Three women, three geese, and three frogs, make a market."

English. "A tailor is the ninth part of a man." *Basque.* "Nine tailors are required to make one man." *Basque.* "A tailor is not a man, he is in fact only a tailor." *

Arabic. "The camel lifted the load and succumbed under the sieve." *English.* "The last straw breaks the camel's back."

English. "Learn to shave on a fool's beard." *Egyptian.* "He learns

---

* The Russian peasants believe tailoring was the first trade, and that when Adam and Eve were expelled from Paradise a German tailor was waiting at its gates to rig them out in decent costume.

to bleed on the head of an orphan." *Arabic.* "Learn to shave on an orphan's head."

Songs also stray; thus the national song "Yankee doodle" was identified in America by Kossuth as a Hungarian tune. It has been traced back in England to the reign of Charles the First and it is still used in the Netherlands by the peasants, and in Biscay as a sword-dance.

THE DECAY OF PROVERBIAL LORE CALLS FOR IMMEDIATE ACTION.

Everywhere and in every country the cry goes up of the decay and gradual disappearance of those finger-posts of the past, Folk-Lore traditions and old customs. To these must be added saws or pithy sayings and proverbs; like the Indians they retire to the forests, they have held their ground in the night of time, but are vanishing with the dawn of book knowledge. The rail is levelling all local knowledge, while education and emigration are sweeping proverbs with their interpretations away into the gulf of oblivion.*

Now or never must be our motto.

> Before Decay's effacing fingers
> Have swept the lines where beauty lingers.

We must now pay special attention to collect the unwritten proverbs, and all saws that throw light on the Anglo-Keltic past and on our eastern affinities. The English Dialect Society was founded with the object of availing itself "of the last chance of saving the fast-fading relics of those forms of Archaic English which have lingered on in country places." The Folk-Lore Society in its department has a similar vocation, and especially with regard to proverbs, in giving not only the proverb but the meaning of it; those dark sayings having often double interpretations.

EXAMPLES SET BY GERMANY AND RUSSIA.

Other nations have set us an example, take for instance the great *Dictionary of German Proverbs*, by Wander, a truly wonderful book.

---

* Old dialects and traditions have been fitly compared to an iceberg drifting into southern latitudes gradually melting beneath the genial sun of civilisation.

The author starts with the principle that "speech is the heart, but proverbs are the veins which send the blood to all parts of the body; proverbs show more than history." The printing was begun in 1866; seven-eighths of it is completed, comprising 45,000 German and 15,000 of foreign origin incorporated into German; it has taken the author sixteen years at twelve hours a day; the book is arranged according to subjects in alphabetical order. We find in it the number of proverbs on the following subjects: the horse 900, the dog 1800, vermin 188, the devil 1700.

Russia has been in the field; Dahl in 1863 published a classified collection of 25,000 Russian proverbs; and in 1868 Masson printed a book "Mudrost Narodnay," or Russian proverbs grouped according to analogy in the German, English, French, Italian, Servian, Latin, Spanish, Polish, while as early as 1834 Snegiref issued in four volume. his Classification of Russian Proverbs. We give the heads of it:

Book 1.

Introduction :
    1. On the foreign sources of Russian proverbs.
    2. On the relation of Russian proverbs to philology.

Book 2.

Anthropological :
    The natural and moral properties connected with various people.
    Proverbs relating to language, faith, superstition, ethics, customs.
    Ethical.

Book 3.

Political, Judicial :
    Legislation.
    Laws.
    Crimes and Punishments.
    Judicial Ceremonies.

Book 4.

Physical Proverbs :
    a. Meteorological, Astrological.

  b. Rural.

  c. Medicinal.

Historical Proverbs:

  a. Chronological.

  b. Topographical.

  c. Ethnographic.

  d. Personal.

  e. Virgins.

I hope that steps will be taken in the course of the year by this Society to prepare a series of volumes of proverbs,—English, Irish, Scotch, Welsh, arranged according to subjects, and annotated.   The classification might be on a plan similar to the following:

Agricultural.	Holy days.
Animals.	Home.
Anthropology.	Hope.
Bureaucracy.	Ignorance.
Chastity.	Industry.
Classes in Society.	Justice.
Clergy and Sects.	Law.
Co-operation.	Landlord, peasant.
Commerce.	Love.
Courage.	Master, servant.
Covetousness.	Matrimonial.
Customs, Change of	Mediæval England.
Death.	Moderation, temperance.
Devil.	Monks.
Doctors.	Morals.
Envy.	National.
Ethnography.	Natural History.
Family.	Opportunity, punctuality.
Gluttony.	Parents.
Gratitude.	Patience.
Health.	Places, persons.
Historical.	Prudence.

Races: Kelts or Ancient Bri-
    tons, Irish, Scotch, Welsh,
    Romans, Saxons, Danes,
    Normans, Gipsies, Jews.
Seasons.
Scriptures.
Social life.

Superstition.
Trades.
Village system.
Weather wisdom.
Wit.
Women.
Youth, age.

Specimens of Anglo-Keltic Proverbs.

The following Anglo-Keltic proverbs are submitted as specimens of the treasures that lie hidden, and which it is very desirable to collect from old MSS. and the mouths of the common people:

Gaelic. "A fish from the river, a tree from the forest, a deer from the mountain, are thefts no man was ever ashamed of." This is a relic of the principle of community of living, once the same in England, India, and Russia.

Breton. " One doer is worth 100 talkers."

Lancashire. " No more use for a book than a duck has for an umbrella."

Lancashire. " Fair and foolish, long and lazy."

Lancashire. " It is a sin to steal a goose from the common,
        But who steals the common from the goose?"
A hit at the Norman lords' and landlords' encroachments on commons.

Lancashire. " One cannot trade without holding a candle to the devil." Tricks of trade.

English. " The friar preached against stealing when he had a pudding in his sleeve."

English. " Like the tailor who sewed for nothing and found thread beside."

English. " Fools build houses, wise men buy them."

English. " A bushel of March dust is worth a Jew's ransom."

English. " Nothing old but shoes and hats."

English. " He who marries a widow has a death's head in his dish."

Scotch. " Count like Jews and agree like brethren."

Scotch. " Daughters and dead fish are no keeping ware."

Scotch. " Do as the lasses do, say no and take it."

Scotch. " He's an Aberdeen man, take his word again."

Scotch. " Nae penny nae paternoster."

Scotch. " They that burn you for a witch lose all their cauls."

Scotch. " Ye look liker a thief than a bishop."

English. " Never let the plough stand to catch a mouse."

English. " An ounce of mother wit is worth a pound of clergy."

English. " Better keep under an old hedge than creep under a new furze bush."

English. " Hope is a good breakfast but a bad supper."

Manx. " Change of work is rest."

Manx. " Learning is fine clothes for the rich man and riches for the poor man."

English. " There is talk of the Turk and the Pope, but it is my next neighbour doeth me the hurt."

English. " The grey mare is the better horse," *i.e.* the wife wears the breeches.

English. "A woman hath nine lives and a cat so many."

English. "A nurse spoils a housewife," *i.e.* she is more daintily fed and more idle.

English. " Put a miller, a tailor, and a weaver in a bag and shake them, the first that cometh out will be a thief."

Breton. " We nourish the cattle from the meadows, the cattle give dung, the dung gives corn."

Welsh. "A servant's friendship is froth."

Welsh. " If you refuse a wife with one fault you will take one with two."

Welsh. " A rope is strong, a maid draws stronger."

Welsh. " In three things a man may be deceived. In a man till known, in a tree till down, in the day till done."

Breton. " One thing you have never seen, a mouse's nest in a cat's ear."

Manx. " Soon ripe, soon rotten."

Manx. " Hit him again, for he is Irish."

Manx. "You must summer and winter a stranger before you can form an opinion of him."

English. " Like Banbury tinkers who in stopping one hole make two."

Breton. " To seek eggs in the nest of the past year."

Breton. " The fox preaching to the geese."

Breton. " A cat in gloves is no use to catch rats."

Breton. " To seek eggs in the nest of last year."

Welsh. " The Welsh know well the Saxon's good will."

FOREIGN PROVERBS FOR COMPARISON WITH ANGLO-KELTIC.

Comparisons bring out the peculiar points of a subject, and the following proverbs of various nationalities are given as specimens with the view of suggesting an inquiry after similar and corresponding ones among Anglo-Keltic proverbs:—

Basque. " Words are females, deeds are males." The Breton has the same.

Afghan. " A spoon proud because porridge has been poured on it."

Polish. " Poland is the peasant's hell, the Jew's paradise, the citizen's purgatory, the noble's heaven, and the grave of the stranger's gold."

Afghan. " If you and I agree what is the lawyer wanted for ?"

Afghan. " If a man said to you a dog has carried away your ear, would you go after the dog or search first for your ear ?"

Basque. " To give to the needy is not to give but to sow."

Telugu. " If the almanacks are lost do the stars also disappear."

Telugu. " Like locking up a bandicoot in a corn-bin."

Turkish. " The knife does not make the cork."

Russ and Spanish. " Take a woman's first advice not her second."

Spanish. " The Jews in their Passover, the Moors in their weddings, the Christians in their law-suits spend much money.

Modern Greek. " My husband does not love me because he does not beat me."

Arabic. " A dog's tail never stands straight."

Servian. " The sun shines on a dirty place but is not dirty."

Polish. " Who goes to Paris an ass does not return a horse."

Basque. " In flying from the wolf he met the bear."

Talmud. " Eight things are difficult to enjoy in abundance, but in moderation are good; labour, sleep, riches, journeyings, love, warm water, bleeding, and wine."

QUESTIONS AND PROPOSALS REGARDING ANGLO-KELTIC PROVERBS.

1. Any proverbs of prehistoric origin referring to prehistoric customs.*

2. Any proverbs of Keltic origin referring to Keltic customs.

3. Any proverbs of Roman origin referring to Roman customs.

4. Any proverbs of Saxon origin referring to Saxon customs.

5. Any proverbs of Danish origin referring to Danish customs.

6. Any proverbs of Norman origin referring to Norman customs.

7. Any proverbs of Scotch origin referring to Scotch customs.

8. Any proverbs on the Gipsies, especially those throwing light on their Indian origin.

9. A Collection of Songs and Proverbs of the Gipsies.†

10. Anglo-Keltic proverbs made by women.‡

11. Anglo-Keltic proverbs unwritten.

12. To obtain the translation of the MS. Irish proverbs in the Royal Irish Academy § with a view to publication.

MEANS FOR COLLECTING ANGLO-KELTIC PROVERBS.

In collecting proverbs in India I found newspaper editors advertised for them, and many came to me in this way. I have lately obtained Gujerat proverbs by the same agency, and I am promised Tamul. Village schoolmasters collected many for me among the peasantry, and I paid women to go and collect them among the women. One of the best collections of Indian proverbs was made by Mr. Thorburn when acting as a Revenue Commissioner. White in his " Selborne " has

---

* I found in Macintosh's Gaelic Proverbs " As dexterous as an Arch-druid." This proverb, like the Baal-fire in June, throws us back on pre-Roman times.

† In Moscow I bought a collection of the songs of the Russian Gipsies, very melodious and thoroughly original.

‡ In Oriental countries men made all the proverbs—is it so in the West, where women had more influence? The Italians say on this, " In man every mortal sin is venial, in woman every venial sin is mortal." Ray attributes to women the proverb, " What is sauce for the goose is sauce for the gander."

§ I saw eighteen MS. collections there.

done much for nature, showing what a country clergyman can do, and the Rev. A. Charles, Vicar of Brockham, has made a very good selection of proverbs recently.

I would propose, therefore, to enlist the services of

1. Country clergy.
2. Village schoolmasters.
3. Provincial newspapers.
4. Ladies. Two young ladies in India, Miss Frere and Miss Stokes, have collected tales from their servants which have been very popular.
5. The Royal Asiatic Society. The Bengal Asiatic Society. The Bombay Asiatic Society. The Directors of Public Instruction in India—for Oriental proverbs.
6. The Society of Antiquaries of England and of Scotland. The Royal Irish Academy. The Highland Society of Scotland. The Cambrian Society.

And that at the Annual Meeting the subject be taken up by forming a sub-committee of the Folk-Lore Society to consider as to the means of collecting and ultimately publishing a classified and annotated collection of English, Irish, Gaelic, Cornish, and Manx proverbs.

J. LONG.

[See *Notices and News* at the end of this volume for proposed action by the Society.]

PROVERBS AND FOLK-LORE

FROM

WILLIAM ELLIS'S "MODERN HUSBANDMAN" (1750).

N accidental reference to this, I think not very common, book, showed me that it contained a good many dialectal words, and I have since been carefully through it and have extracted these for publication by the English Dialect Society. At the same time—and before Mr. Long had given so marked an impetus to the collection of proverbs—I extracted for the Folk-Lore Society such proverbs and folk-lore as I found scattered through the eight volumes, and these I now offer for consideration.

I have almost always excluded such proverbs as are also found in Ray's collection (Bohn's edition), although one or two of such are included for special reasons. Ellis was a farmer at Little Gaddesden, Hertfordshire. In my selection of words for the Dialect Society I purpose to say a little about him; for present purposes it is sufficient to observe that his writings have a very distinct local colouring, and his proverbial expressions are probably in most cases such as were in general use in the neighbourhood of his abode. One or two are hardly proverbs, but still have something about them which may justify their reproduction here.

It may be worth noting that the proverb which in its most usual form refers to the losing of a *ship* for a ha'p'orth a tar, is given twice by Ellis (vol. iv. pt. 1, p. 87, and v. pt. 1, p. 33) as referring to a *sheep*, and twice (vol. iv. pt. 4, pp. 40 and 110) to a hog. Ray gives, " Ne'er lose a hog for a halfpenny-worth of tar," and adds " some have it, lose not a sheep, &c. Indeed, tar is more used about sheep than swine. Others say, lose not a ship," &c. It seems most likely that *sheep*, not *ship*, is the correct reading.

I have arranged some of the proverbs under the following class headings :—*Animals, Birds,* and *Trees and Plants ;* the others are placed under their principal words.

One or two proverbs and scraps of Folk-lore are given from other works of Ellis; these are always specified. When only the volume and page are referred to, the *Modern Husbandman* is intended.

ANIMALS : *Bull.*—See *Cock.*

Calf.—" The old maxim, *Change of pasture makes the calf fat.*"— Vol. iii. pt. 2, p. 44.

Cow.—" About sun-rising they [the Cambridge dairymaids] put the cream into a barrel-churn after they have milked their cows ; for it is a proverb, '*If the cows be not milked by the time the herdsman blows his horn, it spoils the dairymaid's marriage,*' and he blows about sun-rising."—Vol. iii. pt. 1, p. 135.

" A frog put down a cow's throat, and she immediately drove into water, she will p—s clear."—*Practical Farmer,* pp. 126-7.

Dog.—" When a rich miser keeps such a [table] that, according to the old proverbial phrase, ' *The dog may be said to run away with whole shoulders.*' "—Vol. vi. pt. 3, p. 132.

" The proverb says, ' *That a man, a horse, and a dog, are never weary of each others company.*'"—*Shepherd's Guide,* p. 9.

Hog.—" The old saying, ' *That a hog is good for nothing till he is dead.*' "—Vol. vi. pt. 2, p. 79.

Horse.—" The common and true saying, ' *The eye of the master makes the horse fat.*' "—Vol. iii. pt. 2, p. 4.

Cf. " The eye of the master does more than both his hands."— Bohn, p. 503.

In vol. v. pt. 2, pp. 13 and 123, those are spoken of who " scorn to be put out of their old *Dobyn's* path."

" *One may ride a free horse to death.*"·—Vol. vii. pt. 1, p. 65.

BEER.—" As the verse or proverb says—

New beer, new bread, and green wood,
Will make a man's hair grow through his hood."

Vol. i. pt. 1, p. 91.

BEES.—The following well-known proverb I include on account of a local variant which is added to it :

> " A swarm of bees in May is worth a load of hay ;
> But a swarm in July is not worth a fly :

But our country people enlarge the first line, and say—

> A swarm of bees in May
> Is worth a cow and her calf, and a load of hay."

Vol. iii. pt. 1, p. 167.

" It's commonly regarded for a fortunate omen to buy a hive of bees by exchanging a commodity for it of its equal value, or to give gold for it if change is to be returned."—Vol. iv. pt. 1, p. 182.

"All that keep bees should love them, for these hate those that hate them. A farmer's wife loved them much, but her husband hated them ; they would sting him, but not her."—Vol. iv. pt. 2, p. 117.

BIRDS : *Cock.*—" The old verse says :

> He that will have his farm full
> Must keep an old cock and a young bull."

Vol. iii. pt. 1, p. 94.

Owl.—" Adventurous youths are most of them so silly as to disbelieve such a bird as an owl dare attack and wound them, though they provoke them ever so much, according to the old saying commonly made use of by our country Corydons, in their quarrelling disputes, ' *Do you think I was born in a wood to be feared by an owl?* ' "
—Vol. v. pt. 2, p. 103.

The following note on the owl may be worth extracting.

" With us the owl is called *Hobhouchin*, and makes a great hooping noise, or cry, many times in the night, especially in a fair one; for when the owl whoops loudest, and does this oftenest, it is by most deemed a sign of pleasant weather, according to the verse ;

> " ——Nor th' owl foretelling vain,
> From the high roofs, observing Phœbus set,
> Will idly then nocturnal notes repeat."

She will not sing against rain, and has this further observation re-corded of her, that when she frequents a town more than ordinary it presages mortality and sickness to that place ; but according to the notion of country dames it is this screech-owl that forebodes death or sickness in this manner ; for these make a most disagreeable noise sometimes in our villages, and about our houses in the night-time ; one of which has been known to screech so near a window as to disturb a family, and then it is reckoned a fatal omen."—Vol. v. pt. 2, p. 100.

BUYING.—

> "He that buys
> Ought to have a hundred eyes."
>
> Vol. i. pt. 1, p. 127.

CHEAT.—" . . . . the common saying, *no cheat like a country cheat*, because a person is not so apt to suspect so much villany under a low heel and a round frock as, in a city or great town, a well-dressed. sharper."—Vol. i. pt. 1, p. 99; vol. v. pt. 2, p. 109.

MARL.—

> "He that marles sand may buy land ;
> He that marles moss shall suffer no loss ;
> But he that marles clays flings all away."
>
> Vol. iv. pt. 3, p. 139.

MONTHS.—"The first ploughing is begun in April, for they say, '*Better an April sop than a May clot.*'"—Vol. viii. p. 308.

"We say *a dry March, a wet April, and a dry May make plenty.*" —Vol. iii. pt. 2.

> "A dry March, a wet April, a dry May, and a wet June,
> Is commonly said to bring all things in tune."
>
> Vol. iv. pt. 1, p. 50.

RICHES.—"The old maxim, '*That riches beget riches.*'"—*Practical Farmer* (1759), p. 24.

RIME.—"It is an old country saying, '*A great rime year, a good fruit year.*'"—Vol. v. pt. 1, p. 133.

TOM THUMB.—"He was . . . not one of them that regard a serviceable secret like *a tale of Tom Thumb.*"—*Countr Housewife's Family Companion* (1750), p. 15.

TREES AND PLANTS: *Ash.*—" The lop, when green, burns the best of any, which makes the country-folks rhyme it and say, ' *It's fire for a queen.*' "—Vol. vii. pt. 1, p. 62.

The proverb or saying would probably run—

> Ash, when green,
> Is fire for a queen.

Beans.—" It is an ancient but true proverb,

> Sow beans in the mud
> They'll grow like a wood."
>
> Vol. i. pt. 2, p. 9.

This is given by Ray (Bohn, p. 36) with the omission of the article in the second line, by which omission the sense is rendered less obvious.

Sowing beans " is usually done at Candlemas [Feb. 2], according to the rhyming proverb—

> At Candlemas Day
> It's time to sow beans in the clay."
>
> Vol. viii. p. 309.

Beech.—" If a beech-tree is fell'd about Midsummer the wood of it will last three times longer than that fell'd in winter. ' *Beech in summer and oak in winter*' is now become a common saying."— Vol. vii. pt. 2, p. 59.

" The beech, by its large bud, discovers to the countryman about Christmas that there will be a probability of a moist season the succeeding summer."—Vol. viii. p. 102.

Clover.—" It is a most true maxim that where a full crop of clover or other artificial grass has grown the next corn crop will be the better for it. Hence the common saying had its rise, ' *That clover is the mother of corn.*' "—Vol. i. pt. 2, p. 32 ; vol. ii. pt. 1, p. 77.

Oat.—" They say if a drop of rain or dew will hang on an oat at Midsummer there may be a good crop." — *New Experiments in Husbandry for the month of April* (1736), p. 85.

" It is a usual saying, *That a quick man should sow oats and a slow man barley*, by reason oats need not be sown quite so thick as barley.' ' —Vol. ii. pt. 1, p. 34.

Ray-grass, transmutation of.—" It is the opinion of some, that, where Ray-grass grows some years in ground, the same will in time degenerate into a wild bennet or twitch-grass."—Vol. ii. pt. 1, p. 96.

Service Tree (Pyrus torminalis).—" It is reported by our country-people that the cross of our Blessed Redeemer was of this sort of wood."—Vol. vii. pt. 2, p. 178.

Vetch.—Vetches are " a most hardy grain, according to the com-parison of an old saying,

> ' A Thetch will grow through
> The bottom of an old shoe.' "
>
> Vol. viii. p. 242.

Wheat.—" We say, ' *May never goes out without a wheat-ear.*' "— Vol. iii. pt. 2, p. 8.

" A right management must attend the cut-down wheat in the field, for, according to the old saying, ' *A great deal happens sometimes between the field and the barn.*' "—Vol. vi. pt. 1, p. 28.

" It is a true saying, ' *The more furrows, the more corn.*' "—Vol. ii. pt. 1, p. 35.

" It is a rule with the best farmers that an early sowing intitles them to hope for the best crop, for the old saying among them is, ' *Sow early and have corn, sow late and have straw.*' "—Vol. ii. pt. 1, p. 56.

Willow.—This " is said *to buy the horse before the oak will the saddle* " (vol. vii. pt. 1, p. 93) on account of its comparative rapidity of growth.

This proverb appears in this slightly altered form in *Annals of Agriculture*, vi. 528 (1786).—" *The poplar will buy the horse before the oak can buy the saddle.*"

" When one of these sallows gets a body of about a foot diameter, they are then redhearted . . . . If kept dry, [it] is said to last as long as oak, which occasioned the old saying,

> ' Be the oak ne'er so stout,
> The sollar red will wear it out.' "
>
> Vol. vii. pt. 1, p. 98.

WHET.—"Our labouring-men . . . carry two scythes a-piece with them, which every other night they commonly grind. (*A Whet*, say they, *is no let*)."—Vol. iv. pt. 1, p. 94.

This is given by Bohn (p. 141), but the above explanation seems worth insertion. Cfr. " A store is no sore."

The following do not suggest any definite heading:

" The old saying, ' *A bad husbandman has a good crop once in seven years.*' "—Vol. v. pt. 1, p. 126.

This occurs slightly varied in vol. ii. pt. 1, p. 56,. and vol. iii. pt. 1, p. 11.

" *Happy is he who by other men's harms learns to beware.*"—Vol. vi. pt. 1, p. 123.

" As the proverb says, ' *The obstinate man seldom wants woe.*' "—*Practical Farmer* (1759), p. 134.

" *How a farmer starved his cow, and thought it occasioned by witch-craft.* At Bogden, near Huntingdon, lived one S———n L———n, an old penny-father, that would not allow his cattle meat enough ; for want of which they sometimes died, and then he thought them inchanted or bewitched. This old fellow had a cow that had been kept short, and was so very poor that she could not rise when laid down, and he said she was bewitched ; so, to disenchant her, he takes a long stone bottle and puts some of the cow's stale into it, and corked it up very close, and made a great fire, and set the bottle upon it, and blowed the fire very fiercely, and expected the enchantress to come, yet none appeared. At last, the bottle flew in pieces with the heat, and gave a report bigger than a musquet, and cut the witchfinder's nose half off, and mortified his face to that degree that he looks very frightful. After his conjuration he lay for dead after he had received the shots, and scared his family most abominably."—Vol. vi. pt. 2, p. 107.

A great deal of folk-medicine, relating both to human beings and animals, will be found in Ellis's *Country Housewife's Family Companion.* (1750.)

JAMES BRITTEN.

CHRISTMAS MUMMERS IN DORSETSHIRE.

[Read at the Meeting of the Society on 13th April, 1880.]

O the Christmas number of *Notes and Queries* (5th S. ii. 505) I contributed what was little more than the list of the characters in two several performances given by mummers at Chrismastide, in two distinct parishes in the south-west of Dorset, the full rendering of which would necessarily have taken up too much valuable space.

Since then the Folk-Lore Society has sprung into existence, and offers an opportunity of preserving one of the most interesting forms of our national folk-lore—folk-lore, indeed, which before the rapid march of education and beneath the iron hand of the School Board bids fair to rank ere long amongst the things of the past.

As to the derivation of the word "mummer," the principal authorities seem to be agreed. Strutt, in his *Sports and Pastimes* (ed. 1831, p. 251), says: "In the middle ages mummings were very common. *Mumm* is said to be derived from the Danish word *mumme*, or *momme* in Dutch, and signifies disguise in a mask, hence a mummer."

Brand, in his *Popular Antiquities* (ed. 1841, vol. i. p. 250), says that "it is supposed that mummers were originally instituted in imitation of the Sigillaria or Festival Days added to the ancient Saturnalia;" and in a note appended (p. 250), "*Mummer* signifies a masker, one disguised under a vizard; from the Danish *mumme*, or Dutch *momme*. Lipsius tells us in his 44th Epistle, book iii. that *momar*, which is used by the Sicilians for a fool, signifies in French, and in our own language, a person with a mask on."

Again, Fosbroke in his *Encyclopedia of Antiquities* (ed. 1843, vol. ii. p. 668), *sub voce* " Mummers : These were amusements derived from the Saturnalia, and so called from the Danish *mumme*, or Dutch *momme*, disguise in a mask.   Christmas was the grand scene of mumming, and some mummers were disguised like bears, others like unicorns, bringing presents.   They who could not procure masks rubbed their faces with soot or painted them.   In the Christmas mummings the chief aim was to surprise by the oddity of the masks and singularity and splendour of the dresses.   Everything was out of nature and propriety.   They were often attended with an exhibition of gorgeous machinery.   It was an old custom also to have mummeries on Twelfth Night.   They were the common holiday amusements of young people of both sexes ; but by 6 Edward III. the mummers or masqueraders were ordered to be whipped out of London."

So, too, Chambers (*Book of Days,* ed. 1864, vol. ii. p. 739) gives the same derivation.

In Hone's *Every Day Book* (ed. 1866, p. 823) are given the words of a performance that took place at Whitehaven, entitled " Alexander and the King of Egypt ; a mock play, as it is acted by the Mummers every Christmas," which, in two acts, runs to rather more than a hundred lines or verses, and which contains the following characters : —

ALEXANDER.	DOCTOR.
KING OF EGYPT.	ACTORS.
PRINCE GEORGE.	

Again in Brand (p. 251) there appears a neatly executed whole-page engraving of " Riding a Mumming," in which a goodly party, consisting of men, mounted, some on real and some on dummy horses, surrounded by a motley gathering on foot, is depicted about to enter the courtyard of a fine old Tudor house.

In Chambers's *Book of Days* (vol. ii p. 739) is a capital drawing by A. Crowquill, of a " Party of Mummers," with all the orthodox performers represented in character.   The words of the drama (of about seventy lines) there given are stated to have been already printed in *Tales and Traditions of Tenby*, and the characters consisted of,—

OLD FATHER CHRISTMAS.	DOCTOR.
ST. GEORGE.	OLIVER CROMWELL.
TURKISH KNIGHT.	BEELZEBUB.

In *Notes and Queries* (2nd S. xi. 271) "Cuthbert Bede" gives the Worcestershire version of the play of St. George, called the "Mummers' Masque," in which the characters are more numerous than in the ones I have before alluded to, and comprise,—

LITTLE DEVIL-DOUBT.	TURKISH KNIGHT.
OLD FATHER CHRISTMAS.	VALIANT SOLDIER.
THE NOBLE CAPTAIN.	DOCTOR.
KING GEORGE.	BEELZEBUB.
BOLD BONAPARTE.	

In *Notes and Queries* (4th S. x. 487) a correspondent sends a version that obtains in the North of Ireland, in which "the lads dress themselves for the occasion by putting white shirts over their clothes, and wear tall caps of white paper pointed at top, and with the front flat, something like the conventional bishop's mitre, with scraps of gilt and coloured paper pasted on for ornament. They are also provided with swords of hoop iron."

The characters sustained in this version were,—

LEADER.	ST. PATRICK.
ST. GEORGE.	OLIVER CROMWELL.
A TURK.	BEELZEBUB.
DOCTOR.	DEVIL DOUBT.

It concluded with a song of four lines only, in which all joined.

Another correspondent of *Notes and Queries* (5th S. iv. 511) calls attention to the fact that the contents of the *Peace Egg* (the title of a pamphlet published at Sheffield and Leeds, sold and performed only at Christmas time) were almost identical with the old Christmas mummers' play of St. George, as given in Halliwell's *Rhymes and Tales*, pp. 306—310, the *dramatis personæ* consisting of—

FOOL.	PRINCE OF PARADINE.
ST. GEORGE.	KING OF EGYPT.
SLASHER.	HECTOR.
DOCTOR.	DEVIL DOUBT.

Again, in the Christmas number of *Notes and Queries* for last year (5th S. x. 484), a correspondent mentions the capital account given of the Christmas mummers in *The Return of the Native*, by Thomas Hardy, in which the whole scene is put extremely well before the reader. Further, at p. 489, are given the words of a short play, acted at Christmastide in the neighbourhood of Hastings.

Coming nearer to our own subject, the Rev. W. Barnes, ("the Dorset poet,") in his *Grammar and Glossary of the Dorset Dialect*, (published for the Philological Society, 1863) *s. v.* "Mummers," describes them as "a set of youths who go about at Christmas decked with painted paper and tinsel, and act in the houses of those who like to receive them a little drama, mostly, though not always, representing a fight between St. George and a Mohammadan leader; and commemorative therefore of the Holy Wars. One of the characters, with a hump back and bawble, represents old Father Christmas."

And he goes on to say, that "the libretto of the Dorset mummers is much the same as that of the Cornish ones, as given in the specimens of the *Cornish Provincial Dialect*, published 1846."

On referring to this publication of Mr. Sandys, (who wrote under the pseudonymn of "Uncle Jan Treenoodle,") I find that some portions of the dialogue are certainly much the same as that in the earlier parts of my libretti.

In the Cornish play, however, are introduced two characters—the Dragon, who fights with, and is defeated by, St. George—and the king of Egypt's daughter—both of whom are strangers to my versions.

The above description by Mr. Barnes, however, will very fairly apply to my characters; which are again more numerous than the Cornish ones; to which I may add the one I gave in *Notes and Queries*

(5th S. ii. 505,) and which forms the subject of this present paper, where Father Christmas is represented as being sometimes mounted on a wooden horse covered with trappings of dark cloth, from which the old man is generally more than once thrown. The character of his wife, Old Bet, was taken by a boy with a shrill voice, dressed as a very old woman in a black bonnet and red cloak. The rest of the party was decked out as befitted the character each was intended to assume, garnished with bows, coloured strips of paper, caps, sashes, buttons, swords, helmets, &c. The representation of the play concluded with a song.

At the same time I had ventured to claim as peculiar to the Dorsetshire mummers the introduction of the character of " Old Bet," the wife of old Father Christmas, as no other rendering with which I was acquainted had included it, but since then a correspondent of *Notes and Queries* (5th S. iv. 511), writing from Belper, has claimed her also as taking a vigorous part in a representation given by the neighbouring lads in his kitchen.

Another peculiarity to be noticed in the Dorsetshire versions is, that whilst in nearly all the others I have quoted the actors are represented as asking for " room " to perform in, in these, one of the actors assumes the character of " Room " itself.

The two versions I have, and which I now propose to lay before my readers, being performed in the same county, naturally bear, as will be seen, a strong resemblance to each other ; and, indeed, in all the different accounts I have above referred to, an unmistakeable family likeness is visible.

I will now proceed to give the entire rendering of the first version as it was obtained for me some few years ago by an old Dorsetshire lady, who is now dead, and in this the *dramatis personæ* are as follow :—

OLD FATHER CHRISTMAS.	GRACIOUS KING.
ROOM.	GENERAL VALENTINE.
ANTHONY, the Egyptian King.	COLONEL SPRING.
ST. GEORGE.	OLD BETTY.
ST. PATRICK.	DOCTOR.
CAPTAIN BLUSTER.	SERVANT-MAN.

SCENE:—*The servants' hall or kitchen of the mansion or farmhouse
in which the performance is to take place. The actors are grouped
together at the back of the stage, so to speak, and each comes forward as he is required to speak or to fight, and at the conclusion
falls back upon the rest, leaving the stage clear for other disputants
or combatants. This is the "enter" and "exit" of the mummers.*

Enter OLD FATHER CHRISTMAS.

Here comes I, Father Christmas, welcome or welcome not,
I hope Old Father Christmas will never be forgot.
Although it is Old Father Christmas he has but a short time to stay;
I am come to show you pleasure and pass the time away.
I have been far, I have been near,
And now I am come to drink a pot of your Christmas beer;
And if it's not your best,
I hope in heaven your soul will rest.
If it is a pot of your small,
We cannot show you no Christmas at all.
Walk in Room, again I say,
And pray good people clear the way.
Walk in, Room.

Enter ROOM.

God bless you all, ladies and gentlemen,
It's Christmas time, and I am come again.
My name is Room, one sincere and true,
A merry Christmas I wish to you.
King of Egypt is for to display,
A noble champion without delay.
St. Patrick too, a charming Irish youth,
He can fight or dance, or love a girl with truth.
A noble Doctor I do declare, and his surprising tricks bring up the
    rear,
And let the Egyptian King straightway appear.

Enter EGYPTIAN KING.

Here comes I, Anthony, the Egyptian King.
With whose mighty acts all round the globe doth ring ;
No other champion but me excels,
Except St. George, my only son-in-law.
Indeed that wondrous knight whom I so dearly love,
Whose mortal deeds the world dost [well ?] approve,
That hero whom no dragon could affright,
A whole troop of soldiers couldn't stand in sight.
Walk in St. George, his warlike [ardour ?] to display,
And show Great Britain's enemies dismay.
Walk in, St. George.

Enter ST. GEORGE.

Here am I, St. George, an Englishman so stout,
With those mighty warriors I long to have a bout ;
No one could ever picture me the many I have slain,
I long to fight, it's my delight, the battle o'er again.
Come then, you boasting champions,
And hear that in war I doth take pleasure,
I will fight you all, both great and small,
And slay you at my leisure.
Come haste, away, make no delay,
For I'll give you something you won't like,
And like a true-born Englishman
I will fight you on my stumps.
And now the world I do defy,
To injure me before I die.
So now prepare for war, for that is my delight.

Enter ST. PATRICK, *who shakes hands with* ST. GEORGE.

ST. PATRICK.

My worthy friend, how dost thou fare, St. George ?
Answer, my worthy knight.

St. George.

I am glad to find thee here ;
In many a fight that I have been in, travelled far and near,
To find my worthy friend St. Patrick, that man I love so dear.
Four bold warriors have promised me
To meet me here this night to fight.
The challenge did I accept, but they could not me affright.

St. Patrick,

I will always stand by that man that did me first enlarge,
I thank thee now in gratitude, my worthy friend St. Geärge ;
Thou dids't first deliver me out of this wretched den,
And now I have my liberty I thank thee once again.

Enter Captain Bluster.

I'll give St. George a thrashing, I'll make him sick and sore,
And if 1 further am disposed I'll thrash a dozen more.

St. Patrick.

Large words, my worthy friend,
St. George is here.
And likewise St. Patrick too ;
And he doth scorn such men as you.
I am the match for thee,
Therefore prepare yourself to fight with me,
Or else I'll slay thee instantly.

Captain Bluster.

Come on, my boy !   I'll die before
I yield to thee or twenty more.
        [*They fight, and* St. Patrick *kills* Captain Bluster.]

St. Patrick.

Now one of St. George's foes is killed by me,
Who fought the battle o'er,
And now for the sake of good St. George,
I'll freely fight a hundred more.

ST. GEORGE.

No, no, my worthy friend,
St. George is here,
I'll fight the other three ;
And after that with Christmas beer
So merry we will be.

Enter GRACIOUS KING.

No beer or brandy, Sir, I want my courage for to rise,
I only want to meet St. George or take him by surprise ;
But I am afraid he never will fight me,
I wish I could that villain see.

ST. GEORGE.

Tremble, thou tyrant, for all thy sin that's past,
Tremble to think that this night will be thy last.
Thy conquering arms shall quickly by thee lay alone,
And send thee passing to eternal doom.
St. George will make thy armour ring ;
St. George will soon despatch the Gracious King.

GRACIOUS KING.

I'll die before I yield to thee or twenty more.
    [*They fight*, ST. GEORGE *kills the* GRACIOUS KING.]

Enter General VALENTINE.

ST. GEORGE.

He was no match for me, he quickly fell.

General VALENTINE.

But I am thy match, and that my sword shall tell,
Prepare thyself to die and bid thy friends farewell.
I long to fight such a brave man as thee,
For its a pleasure to fight so manfully.

    *   *   *   * †

Rations so severe he never long to deceive [receive?]
So cruel ! for thy foes [are ?] always killed ;
Oh! what a sight of blood St. George has spilled !

      † Line missing.

I'll fight St. George the hero here,
Before I sleep this night.
Come on my boy, I'll die before
I yield to thee or twenty more.
St. George, thou and I'll the battle try,
If thou dost conquer I will die.

[*They fight.* St. GEORGE *kills the General.*]

St. GEORGE.

Where now is Colonel Spring?   He doth so long delay,
That hero of renown, I long to show him play.

Enter Colonel SPRING.

Holloa! behold me, here am I!
I'll have thee now prepare,
And by this arm thou'lt surely die—
I'll have thee this night beware.
So see what bloody works thou'st made,
Thou art a butcher, Sir, by trade.
I'll kill, as thou didst [kill?] my brother,
For one good turn deserves another.

St. GEORGE.

Come, give me leave, I'll thee battle,
And quickly make thy bones to rattle.

Colonel SPRING.

Come on my boy, I'll die before
I'll yield to thee or twenty more.
St. George, so thee and I
Will the battle try.

[*They fight.* St. GEORGE *kills the* COLONEL.]

St. PATRICK.

Stay thy hand, St. George, and slay no more; for I feel for the
wives and families of those men that you have slain.

St. GEORGE.

So am I sorry. I'll freely give any sum of money to a doctor to restore them again. I have heard talk of a mill to grind old men young, but I never heard of a doctor to bring dead men to life again.

St. Patrick.

There's an Irish doctor, a townsman of mine, who lived next door to St. Patrick, he can perform wonders. Shall I call him, St. George?

St. George.

With all my heart. Please to walk in Mr. Martin Dennis.

Its an ill wind that blows no good work for the doctor.

[*Enter* Doctor.]

If you will set these men on their pins, I'll give thee a hundred pound, and here is the money.

Doctor.

So I will my worthy knight, and then I shall not want for whiskey for one twelvemonth to come. I am sure the first man I saw beheaded, I put his head on the wrong way. I put his mouth where his poll ought to be, and he's exhibited in a wondering nature.

St. George.

Very good answer, Mr. Doctor. Tell me the rest of your miracles and raise those warriors.

Doctor.

I can cure love-sick maidens, jealous husbands, squalling wives, brandy-drinking dames, with one touch of my pepble [triple?] liquid, or one sly dose of my Jerusalem balsam, and that will make an old crippled dame dance the hornpipe, or an old woman of seventy years of age conceive and bear a twin. And now to convince you all of my exertions, rise Captain Bluster, Gracious King, General Valentine, and Colonel Spring! Rise, and go to your father!

[*On the application of the medicine they all rise and retire.*]

Enter Old Bet.

Here comes I dame Dorothy,
A handsome young woman, good morning to ye.
I am rather fat but not very tall,
I'll do my best endeavour to please you all.

My husband he is to work and soon he will return,
And something for our supper bring,
And perhaps some wood to burn.
Oh! here he comes !

[*Enter* JAN *or* OLD FATHER CHRISTMAS.]

Well ! Jan.

OLD FATHER CHRISTMAS.

Oh! Dorothy!

OLD BET.

What have you been doing all this long day, Jan ?

OLD FATHER CHRISTMAS.

I have been a hunting, Bet.

OLD BET.

The devil a hunting is it ! Is that the way to support a wife ? Well, what have you catched to-day, Jan ?

OLD FATHER CHRISTMAS.

A fine jack hare, and I intend to have him a-fried for supper; and here is some wood to dress him.

OLD BET.

Fried ! no, Jan, I'll roast it nice.

OLD FATHER CHRISTMAS

I say I'll have it fried.

OLD BET.

Was there ever such a foolish dish !

OLD FATHER CHRISTMAS.

No matter for that. I'll have it a-done; and if you don't do as I do bid, I'll hit you in the head.

OLD BET.

You may do as you like for all I do care,
I'll never fry a dry Jack hare.

OLD FATHER CHRISTMAS.

Oh ! you won't, wooll'ee ? [will you]

[*He strikes her, and she falls.*]

Oh ! what have I done !   I have murdered my wife !

The joy of my heart, and the pride of my life.

And out to the gaol I quickly shall be sent.

In a passion I did it, and no malice meant.

Is there a doctor that can restore ?

Fifty pounds I'll give him, or twice fifty more.

[*Some one speaks.*]

Oh ! yes, Uncle Jan, there is a doctor just below, and for God's sake let him just come in.   Walk in, Doctor.

Enter DOCTOR.

OLD FATHER CHRISTMAS.

Are you a doctor ?

DOCTOR.

Yes, I am a doctor—a doctor of good fame.   I have travelled through Europe, Asia, Africa, and America, and by long practice and experience I have learned the best of cures for most disorders instant [incident ?] to the human body ; find nothing difficult in restoring a limb, or mortification, or an arm being cut off by a sword, or a head being struck off by a cannon ball, if application have not been delayed till it is too late.

OLD FATHER CHRISTMAS.

You are the very man, I plainly see,

That can restore my poor old wife to me.

Pray tell me thy lowest fee.

DOCTOR.

A hundred guineas I'll have to restore thy wife.

'Tis no wonder that you could not bring the dead to life.

OLD FATHER CHRISTMAS.

That's a large sum of money for a dead wife !

DOCTOR.

Small sum of money to save a man from the gallows. Pray what big stick is that you have in your hand?

OLD FATHER CHRISTMAS.

That is my hunting-pole.

DOCTOR.

Put aside your hunting-pole, and get some assistance to help up your wife.

[OLD BET *is raised up to life again.*]

OLD FATHER CHRISTMAS.

Fal, dal, lal! fal, dal, lal! my wife's alive!

Enter SERVANT-MAN, *who sings.*

Well met, my brother dear!
All on the highway
Sall and I were a walking along,
So I pray come tell to me
What calling you might be ;
I'll have you for some servant-man.

OLD FATHER CHRISTMAS.

I'll give thee many thanks,
And I'll quit thee as soon as I can;
Vain did I know
Where thee could do so or no,
For to the pleasure of a servant-man.

SERVANT-MAN.

Some servants of pleasure
Will pass time out of measure,
With our hares and hounds
They will make the hills and valleys sound ;
That's a pleasure for some servant-man.

OLD FATHER CHRISTMAS.

My pleasure is more than for to see my oxen grow fat,
And see them prove well in their kind,
A good rick of hay and a good stack of corn to fill up my barn,
That's a pleasure of a good honest husbandman.

SERVANT-MAN.

Next to church they will go with their livery fine and gay,
With their cocked-up hat and gold lace all round,
And their shirt so white as milk,
And stitched so fine as silk,
That's a habit for a servant-man.

OLD FATHER CHRISTMAS.

Don't tell I about thee silks and garments that not fit to travel
the bushes.
Let I have on my old leather coat,
And in my purse a groat,
And there, that's a habit for a good old husbandman.

SERVANT-MAN.

Some servant-men doth eat
The very best of meat,
A cock, goose, capon, and swan ;
After lords and ladies dine,
We'll drink strong beer, ale, and wine ;
That's a diet for some servant-man.

OLD FATHER CHRISTMAS.

Don't tell I of the cock, goose, or capon, nor swan ; let I have a
good rusty piece of bacon, pickled pork, in the house, and a hard
crust of bread and cheese once now and then ; that's a diet for a good
old honest husbandman.
So we need must confess
That your calling is the best,
And we will give you the uppermost hand ;

So no more we won't delay,
But we will pray both night and day,
God bless the honest husbandman.
    Amen.   *[Exeunt* OMNES.]

The second version, which I will now give, appears to me to be useful not only in showing the difference in the characters themselves that exists in a representation that must have taken place almost side by side with the other, but also in affording here and there a few words of the old Dorset vernacular, to which I have added a *translation* in a parenthesis, for the benefit of those readers of the " Folk-Lore Record" who may not have met with the words before.

The *dramatis personæ* are as follows :

OLD FATHER CHRISTMAS.	VALIANT SOLDIER.
ROOM.	CUTTING STAR.
TURKISH KNIGHT.	DOCTOR.
KING GEORGE.	OLD BET.
MARSHALEE.	

Enter OLD FATHER CHRISTMAS.

Here comes I, old Father Christmas,
Welcome or welcome not ;
I hope Old Father Christmas will never be forgot.
Now, ladies and gentlemen, if you do not believe what I say,
Walk in my son, Room, and boldly clear the way.

Enter ROOM.

Here comes I, gallant Room, pray give me room to enter,
For I have brought some sport to while away the winter ;
An old act, a new act, an act that was never acted before,
Since I left my poor old grey-headed grandfather down at my old
    back door.
If you do not believe what I say,
Walk in Turkish Knight and boldly clear the way.

TURKISH KNIGHT.

Here comes I that Turkish Knight,
Just come from that Turkish land to fight;
If King George do meet me here,
I will try his courage without fear.

KING GEORGE.

Here comes I, King George,
With my glittering sword and spear;
I fought the dragon boldly and brought him to the slaughter,
But 'twas thus I gained the fairest maid of all, the King of Egypt's
  daughter.

TURKISH KNIGHT.

I pray, King George, do not make so bold,
If thy blood is hot, I will soon make it cold.

KING GEORGE.

My blood is hot as any fire,
And so cold as any clay,
And with my glittering sword and spear,
I'll take thy life away.

TURKISH KNIGHT.

Thee and I will a battle try.

KING GEORGE.

If I conquer, thou must die.
          [*They fight.* TURKISH KNIGHT *is killed.*]
Thy first son, Old Father, is dead ;
Call in thy second son Marshalee, that champion whom I dread.

Enter MARSHALEE.

Here comes I Marshalee,
I am the man who will conquer thee;

My head is lined with iron,
My body is lined with steel,
I will fight thee, King George,
If it is not against thy will.

KING GEORGE.

If it's not against thy will, Marshalee,
Or yet against thy might;
If thou could'st fight against King George,
Then draw thy sword and fight ?
        [*They fight.*   MARSHALEE *is wounded.*]
Thy second son, Old Father, is wounded;
Call in thy third son, the Valiant Soldier.

Enter VALIANT SOLDIER.

Here comes I, that Valiant Soldier,
Slasher is my name;
With sword and pistol by my side
I hope to win the game.
One of my brothers I have seen wounded,
And another I have seen slain;
I'll fight thee, King George,
On the British plain.

KING GEORGE.

Thee and I will a battle try.

VALIANT SOLDIER.

If I conquer, thou must die.
        [*They fight.*   VALIANT SOLDIER *falls wounded.*]

KING GEORGE.

Thy third son, Old Father, is wounded;
Call in thy fourth son, the Cutting Star,
That champion whom I dread.

Enter CUTTING STAR.

Where is King George, that champion bold?
If his blood is hot, I will soon have it cold.

KING GEORGE.

Here am I, King George.   I am come here,
And will try thy courage without fear.

CUTTING STAR.

Here comes I, the Cutting Star,
Just come from that dreadful war;
I have fought many a battle with the French,
And come to encounter thee, King George, so bold.

KING GEORGE.

Thee and I will a battle try.

CUTTING STAR.

If I conquer, thou must dié.
                    [*They fight.*   CUTTING STAR *falls.*]

KING GEORGE.

I have a little bottle by my side called the Liptupain; [?.
If that soldier is alive, let him rise and fight again.

TURKISH KNIGHT.

Oh ! pardon me, King George.   Oh ! pardon me, I crave ;
Pardon me this night, and I will be thy slave.

KING GEORGE.

I never will pardon thee, Turkish Knight ;
Therefore rise thou, Turkish Knight,
Draw thy sword, and we will fight.

ROOM.

Hold thy hand, butcher, and kill no more,
For I fear for their poor wives and families.

KING GEORGE.

Are you the brother of these dead men
That lie bleeding on the ground?

ROOM.

Yes, I am, and come to try thy might.

KING GEORGE.

If you are come to try my might,
Draw thy purse and pay thy part:
And draw thy sword and we will fight.

OLD FATHER CHRISTMAS.

What wild moans and wild groans there are in the field of battle!
Is there a doctor to be found
Can rise these dead men from the ground,
And have them for to stand?

KING GEORGE.

Yes, Father, there is a doctor to be found
Can rise these dead men from the ground,
And bring them for to stand.

FATHER CHRISTMAS.

Doctor! Doctor! Doctor!
You had better call him, King George.

KING GEORGE.

I will warrant he will answer to my first call.   Doctor!

DOCTOR.

Oh yes! Father, there is a doctor to be found,
Can rise these dead men from the ground,
And have them for to stand.

FATHER CHRISTMAS.

What canst thou cure?

DOCTOR.

I can cure the itch, the stitch, the palsy, and the gout,
All pains in, and all pains out,
And if the devil is in thy sons,
I will quickly pull him out.

FATHER CHRISTMAS.

What's thee [thy?] fees?

DOCTOR.

Fifty poun', Father.

FATHER CHRISTMAS.

What's say, half-crown?

DOCTOR.

Fifty poun', Father.

FATHER CHRISTMAS.

I ain't got so much money as that.

DOCTOR.

I can't do it no less.

FATHER CHRISTMAS.

Nory [ne'er a] trifle less at all?

DOCTOR.

Fifty poun' is my fee,
But ten less, I'll take of thee.

FATHER CHRISTMAS.

Try thee skill.

DOCTOR.

I have a little bottle by my side, called the dicky-whip [?]
I put a drop to each soldier's heart,
Rise! Champions, rise! and all pay your part.

FATHER CHRISTMAS.

I have travelled o'er hills and valleys where the winds never blow,
nor the cock never crow, nor the Devil never sound his horn-pipe.

That was never in your time, and nobody else's time; time when little
birds used to build in old man's beards, but ain't got norry [ne'er a]
one in mine yet.

King GEORGE.

I've heard a great deal about your old travels.   Did you never get a
partiner? [partner.]

Father CHRISTMAS.

I should think I did.

King GEORGE.

What may your partiner's name be?

Father CHRISTMAS.

Old Bet.

King GEORGE.

Call her in, in the old fashion—Bet—

Father CHRISTMAS.

Bet! Bet! Bet!

King GEORGE.

Call her a little louder.

Father CHRISTMAS.

I wish you to call her, King George.

King GEORGE.

Dorothy Dame!

Enter OLD BET.

Here comes I, little Dame Dorothy,
I wish you all a very good morrety [morn t'ye].
My head is big, my body is small,
I'll endeavour my best to please you all.

Father CHRISTMAS.

Wher'st thou been, Bet?

BET.

In the land of Nod, John,
Where there's devil, man, nor dog, John.

Father CHRISTMAS.

Dissen [didn't ye] see nobody at all there, Bet?

BET.

No, John, only an old man chewing baccy.

Father CHRISTMAS.

Didener [didn't he] gee [give] thee norry [ne'er a] quid, Bet ?

BET.

Yes, John.

Father CHRISTMAS.

Where's my sher [share] ?

BET.

Up in higher cupboard.

Father CHRISTMAS.

Not there, Bet.

BET.

Down in lower cupboard.

Father CHRISTMAS.

Tidden ['tisn't] there, Bet.   Oh ! you lying old hag !

BET.

I have fired it through a nine-inch wall, knocked down a puppy dog ; hear 'un say " bow wow " nine times aäder [after] he was dead.

> [FATHER CHRISTMAS, *enraged, beats* BET *round the house, and finally kills her.*]

FATHER CHRISTMAS.

What wild moans and wild groans there are in a field of battle !
Is there any doctor to be found
Can rise my dead wife from the ground,
And bring her for to stand?

KING GEORGE.

Oh ! yes, there is a doctor to be found,
Can rise your dead wife from the ground,
And bring her for to stand.

FATHER CHRISTMAS.

Doctor ! doctor ! doctor !

KING GEORGE.

Call her a little louder, Father.

FATHER CHRISTMAS.

Doctor ! doctor ! doctor ! doctor !
I can't call him any louder.   You call him, King George.

KING GEORGE.

Doctor !

Enter DOCTOR.

Yes, Father, there is a doctor to be found
Can rise your dead wife from the ground,
And have her for to stand.

FATHER CHRISTMAS.

What canst cure ?

DOCTOR.

I can cure the itch, the stitch, the palsy, and the gout,
All pains in and all pains out ;
And if the old man is in thy wife I'll quickly turn him out.

FATHER CHRISTMAS.

What's thee [thy] fees ?

DOCTOR.

Fifty poun', father.

FATHER CHRISTMAS.

I ain't got so much money as that.

DOCTOR.

Fifty poun' is my fee,
Father, but ten less I'll take of thee.

FATHER CHRISTMAS.

Can't you cure norry [ne'er a] bit more?

DOCTOR.

Yes, Father, all young women that have the heartache, give them a
pill of mine,
That will set them all right in a decline.

FATHER CHRISTMAS.

Cans't thou rise my dead wife from the ground?

DOCTOR.

Bleed her in the eye vein, Father.

[FATHER CHRISTMAS *goes to her feet, and then to her head to bleed
her feet.*]
Now, Bet, dance with John?

[BET *gets up.*]

FATHER CHRISTMAS.

Fal the dal! my wife's alive;
Where's thee ben [been] to, Bet?

BET.

Where's thee ben to, John?

FATHER CHRISTMAS.

Ich ben [I've been] hunting.

BET.

What'st catched, John?

FATHER CHRISTMAS.

Wold [old] dry Jack hare.

BET.

Howse [How are you] going haven [have it] cooked, John?

FATHER CHRISTMAS.

I shall haven fried.

BET.

I shall haven griddled [grilled].

FATHER CHRISTMAS.

I shall haven fried.

BET.

I shall never have a wold [old] Jack hare fried.

FATHER CHRISTMAS.

Goo [go] and get the hobby-hoss, Bet.

[*The hobby-horse is brought in, upon which* FATHER CHRISTMAS *mounts.*]

DOCTOR.

Now, ladies and gentlemen, you can plainly see that I am not one of these Italian doctors running from door to door, telling a pack of lies, for I can cure the sick and rise the dead right plain before your eyes, and bring them for to stand.

[*Here follows a Song, after which exeunt* OMNES.]

The play over, and the actors regaled with such good cheer as the hospitable hearts of the Dorsetshire folk seldom refused, the Mummers passed on to the next parish, where to a fresh and ever-delighted audience they went through a repetition of their performance; and though, if the night were wet, and the wind cold, they experienced rough usage at times, yet their welcome was all the warmer at their next halting-place, so that none could doubt for a moment but that they came in for no small share of the delights of a " merry Christmas."

J. S. UDAL.

Inner Temple.

[An interesting discussion followed the reading of Mr. Udal's paper, and among the notes since handed in to the honorary secretary the following seem to give some useful additional material and comments.

(*a*) Mr. J. T. Mickethwaite, F.S.A. handed in a " chap-book " copy of " The Peace Egg " play mentioned on page 3, which gives the character of Beelzebub in addition to those mentioned by Mr. Udal. It is printed at " London and Otley " (Yorkshire), for " William Walker and Sons." n. d. Mr. Micklethwaite also handed in an account of a Mummery play taken down verbally by Miss Wedgewood at Dumbleton, near Evesham, in Gloucestershire. It has been acted at Dumbleton from time immemorial, and, there being no written record of the play, it has been handed down by memory from year to year. The Mummers get themselves up in any light-coloured articles, and they all always wear a high sugar-loaf hat covered with ends of ribbon, &c. The characters are—

FATHER CHRISTMAS.	DOCTOR.
ST. GEORGE.	JACK FINNY.
DUKE WELLINGTON.	SAUCY JACK.

This play differs from the others in that St. George, in fighting with Duke Wellington, gets wounded and beaten instead of himself being victorious, and the doctor is called in, with the same incidents as in the other plays, to cure him. This may, perhaps, be a late adaptation to suit the popular estimate of the Duke of Wellington's prowess as a commander, but it has the same kind of language as the plays in other parts of the country.

(*b*) Mrs. Nina Sharp writes as follows :—

I was staying at Minety, near Malmesbury, in Wilts, (my cousin is the vicar) when the mummers came round (1876). They went through a dancing fight in two lines opposed to each other—performed by the Seven Champions of Christendom. There was no St. George, and they did not appear to have heard of the Dragon. When I inquired for him, they went through the performance of drawing a tooth—the tooth produced, after great agony, being a horse's. The Mummers then carried into the hall a bush gaily decorated with coloured ribbons, and the ladies present were asked to tie on more pieces, which we did, my cousin's wife having previously collected a supply. They then offered a very old, curiously carved, cocoa-nut cup, into which we each put a piece of money. The cup was then filled with beer for each Mummer. These men were of the better class of farm-servants, and were all in white smock-frocks and masks. They sang very well together, especially a ballad (modern ?) about a Lancashire Lass

> " With the little blue handkerchief
> Tied under her chin."

At Acomb, near York, I saw very similar Mummers a few years ago. They went through the same performance of the Seven Champions, but they distinguished St. George, and the Dragon was a prominent person. There was the same tooth-drawing, and I think the Dragon was the patient, and was brought back to life by the operation. One of the carols they sang was the well-known one about the " Seven Joys and Sorrows of Mary."

(c) Mr. Alfred Nutt suggests that the incidents of the mumming-plays were those common to Folk-Tales all over Europe. There were the two heroes, of whom the weaker first engages in combat: the stronger one (in this case St. George, the hero of the Goldenlocks cycle of Folk-Tales in so many European countries) then overcomes three successive champions. This threefold combat is especially characteristic of Celtic Folk-Tale. So, too, is the life-restoring leech (stated in the play to be an *Irishman*), who is met with in the *Mabinogion* and in Campbell's *Popular Tales*, and whose special function it is to bring back to life the champions slain by the hero. The final fight between Father Christmas and Old Bet may possibly be a reminiscence of the struggle for the magic fish or beast between Ceridwen and Gwion in the *Mabinogion*, between Fionn and his foster-father in the Ossianic *Heldensage*, and between Sir James Ramsay or Sir Patrick Farquhar and the magician in Gaelic Folk-Tale. It would be interesting to find Folk-Tale incidents of a specially Celtic nature existing in a genuine English county, one too where the Folk-Tale itself had probably been long extinct.

(*d*) Mr. Hyde Clarke writes : The mask is found in all epochs and in every region.   Although in the present day simply a disguise in Europe, that is not its original or sole reference.   In the tombs golden masks are found, and in Egyptian burials outside reproductions of the face of the deceased.   There is reason to associate the mask with the Ka, or incorporeal double of the body, of higher functions and more sacred character.   This is the foundation of our own superstition of what in life is the fetch of a man, and after death the ghost.   The mask is a characteristic of sacred and popular festivals. It is thus that it becomes traditionally associated with mumming, though in our day not an essential.   The form of the mummings laid before us is necessarily adapted to the epoch at which it was assumed, and when it replaced some older form.   The great event of the Crusades determined this shape as it affected many institutions, and thus St. George appears as a main figure among modern and incongruous accessories.   The introduction of St. Patrick is quite modern, and, though taken from the Seven Champions of Christendom, is a recent compliment to the Irish comrades of the village veterans who had served in the wars.   The doctor is adopted from the itinerant charlatans of the fair and market.   The language is worked up for each character by the village authority who succeeds to its impersonation, and this is well paralleled in stage history by the Italian and French harlequinade, where the harlequin, pantaloon, or other personage worked in the lines of the character in his own fashion.   Thus at one period in this country each village or group of villages had its own mummers, and each town its body of performers of miracle plays.   Thus a corps of popular actors existed, and it is this which in course of time supplied the manipulators of the puppet-shows, of Punch and Judy, and of our pantomimes. Punch and Judy, it will be seen on comparison, is only an English form, and an epitome of the mumming.   One of the changes of our epoch in connection with Folk-Lore is the extinction of this popular or unwritten drama—just as we lose that of the ballad and the epic, as indeed we lose the tale-teller and the fairy tale.   The paper before us is therefore of particular value in exhibiting the last forms of a dying institution, and appropriate as an illustration of the lore of St. George at the period of the annual festival of the national patron.

(e) Mr. James Britten writes: In Patrick Kennedy's *Banks of the Boro*, pp. 226-229 (1867), there is a Wexford mumming-play which is in the main similar to those given by Mr. Udal. The *dramatis personæ* are—St. George, St. Patrick, Oliver Cromwell, a doctor, Beelzebub, and Devil D'Out. Mr. Kennedy's *Fireside Stories of Ireland* have been already referred to in the *Folk-Lore Record*, vol. ii. pp. 18, 224, in complimentary terms. Some of our Members will be glad to know that his *Banks of the Boro* and *Evenings in the Duffrey* contain a great deal of Folk-Lore relating to the county Wexford. Messrs. Gill, of Sackville Street, Dublin, publish a cheap issue of each at 1*s.* 6*d.*

(*f*) In addition to the derivations of the word "mummer" noted by Mr. Udal, that given in the *Promptorium Parvulorum* is worth recording. "Mummynge; *mussacio, vel mussatus.* Mummynge seems to have denoted originally a dumb show, a pantomime, performed by masked actors, a Christmas diversion. 'Mummar, *mommevr.* I mumme in a mummynge. Let vs go mumme (mummer) to nyght in womens apparayle.'—Palsg. 'Compare Dutch mumme, Ger. momme, *larva,* Fr. momme, mascarade, déguisement.'—Roquef. 'Mommon, a troupe of mummers; also, a visard or mask; also, a set, by a mummer, at dice.'—Cotg." (p. 348)—Ed.].

INDIAN MOTHER-WORSHIP.

[Reprinted from *The Athenæum* of December 6th, 1879, pp. 727-8, with a note by Henry Charles Coote, F.S.A.]

NE of the most remarkable features of the multiform and many-sided Hindu religion is the efficacy supposed to belong to the worship of divine Mothers. This idea probably had its origin in the patriarchal constitution of ancient Aryan society. Among the early Aryans the paternal and maternal tie, and, indeed, the whole family bond, was intensely strong. If the father was regarded with awe as the primary source of life, the mother was an object of devotion to the children of the family as the more evident author of their existence. And again, if the father was venerated as the food supplier and protector (*pitā*), the mother was beloved as the meter out (*mātā*) of daily nourishment—the arranger of the household, measuring and ordering its affairs as the moon (also called *mātā*) measured the time. To the Aryan family the father and mother were present gods.

Can we wonder that with the growth of devotional ideas and the increasing sense of a higher superintending providence the earliest religious creed was constructed on what may be called paternal and maternal lines? At first the sky (Dyaus, Zeus), bending over all, was personified as a Heavenly Father (Dyaus-pitar, Jupiter), and the Earth as the Mother of all creatures. Then, in place of the Earth, Infinite Space (*A-diti*) was thought of as an eternal Mother. Then Prakriti was the germinal productive principle—the eternal Mother capable of evolving all created things out of herself, but never so creating unless united with the eternal spiritual principle called the eternal Male (Purusha).

To the prevalence of such ideas must, I think, be attributed the fact that everywhere throughout India are scattered shrines which on inspection are found to contain no images or idols shaped like human beings, but simply stone symbols of a double form, intended to typify the blending of the male and female principles in creation. The casual tourist, whose notions of propriety are cast in a European mould, is shocked by what he considers an evidence of the utter degradation of Indian thought. He turns away in disgust, and denounces the Hindu religion as simple abomination.

My own researches into Indian religious thought have led me to view in these symbols a proof of the hold which the ancient dualistic philosophy has on the Hindu mind. It is common to say that Brahmanism is pure pantheism: it is quite as frequently pure dualism. Vast numbers of Indian thinkers believe that there are two distinct eternally existing essences, and that these are united in the work of creation. To any one imbued with such philosophical conceptions the Lingam and the Yoni are suggestive of no improper ideas. They are either types of the two mysterious creative forces, the efficient and material causes of the universe, or symbols of one divine power delegating procreative energy to male and female organisms. They are mystical representatives, and perhaps the best possible impersonal representatives, of the abstract expressions paternity and maternity.

Of course, such ideas are too mystical and philosophical for the masses of the people. Yet the ordinary Hindu finds no difficulty in accepting the theory of a universe proceeding from a divine father and mother. Hence some images of S'iva (called *Ardha nári*) represented him as male on one side of his body and female on the other, to indicate that he combines in his own person maternal as well as paternal qualities and attributes. It is a mistake to describe the god S'iva as the destroying deity. When he presides over dissolution, he does so in another capacity and under another name. As S'iva he is simply the eternal reproducer, and all the mothers of India are simply manifestations of portions of his essence. They are variously classified, according to various degrees of participation in the god's energy—such as the full, the partial, and the still more partial—the highest being identified with different forms of his supposed consort, the lowest including human mothers in different degrees from Brāhman mothers downwards, who are all worshipped as incarnations of the one divine productive capacity of nature. In fact, Mother-worship in some form or other is the popular worship of India. In the first place, every living mother is venerated as a kind of deity by her children. Then almost every village has its own special guardian Mother, called Mātā or Ambā, or in the south of India Amman. Generally there is also a male guardian deity, who protects, like the female, from all adverse and demoniacal influences. The popular male god is Ganes'a, and in the south of India Ayenār, who rides round the fields every night on horseback, and has clay horses round his shrine. But the Mother is the favourite object of adoration; she is more easily propitiated by prayer, flattery, and offerings, more ready to defend from evil, more dangerously spiteful and prone to inflict diseases if offended by neglect.

There are about one hundred and forty distinct Mothers in Gujarāt, declared by the Brāhmans to be different forms of S'iva's consort. They are really the representatives of ancient local deities (Grāma-devatās), worshipped by the inhabitants from time immemorial. Some are represented by rudely-carved images, others by simple symbols, and others are remarkable for preferring empty shrines and the absence of all visible representation. I visited a small village near Kaira presided over by a Mother worshipped under the name Khodiyar (Mischief), because she is supposed when in an amiable mood to shield from harm. Nor is she undeserving of her name, for she will turn mischievous when her temper is ruffled by neglect. If an epidemic breaks out among the villagers Mother Mischief is believed to be offended, and must be appeased by extraordinary offerings, and perhaps by blood. Another Mother in a neighbouring village is worshipped under the name Untāi. She has the special function of preventing or producing cough in children. Another, named Berāi, prevents cholera; another, called Marakī (popularly Markī), causes cholera; another, Hadakāī, controls mad dogs and prevents hydrophobia; another, As'ā-purī, represented by two idols, satisfies the hopes of wives by giving children. A popular Mother in the west of India, called Becharā-jī, is sometimes represented by a coloured square figure, divided by lines into six compartments. Not a few are worshipped either as causing or protecting from witchcraft and demoniacal possession. The offering of goats' blood to some of these Mothers is supposed to be very effectual; the animals are not always killed. A story is told of a clever Hindu doctor who cured a whole village of influenza by simply assembling the inhabitants and solemnly letting loose a pair of scapegoats into a neighbouring wood infested by demons. The Mothers in some places are themselves demons; for example, Pidārī, Kūterī, and Kulumāndī in Southern India. Blood is their food, and if not supplied with blood they take the life of human beings. When a woman dies unpurified within fifteen days after childbirth she becomes a demon called Churel. She is then always on the watch to attack other young mothers.

On the other hand, the power of at least one well-disposed Mother in Gujarāt is exerted in a remarkable way for the benefit of women after childbirth. Among a very low-caste set of basket-makers (called Pomlā) it is the usual practice of a wife to go about her work immediately after delivery, as if nothing had happened. The presiding Mātā of the tribe is supposed to transfer her weakness to her husband, who takes to his bed and has to be supported for several days with good nourishing food.

Perhaps the most commonly propitiated Mother is S'ītalā, often called Devī, "the goddess," and in the south of India Māriamman. She presides over small-pox, and may prevent small-pox, cause small-pox, or be herself small-pox. Hence the bodies of those who die of small-pox are not burned but buried, lest in burning the corpse the crime of burning the very essence of the goddess herself should be perpetrated. The eight Mothers worshipped by the Tāntrikas of Bengal are each represented with a child in her lap, and it is remarkable that the goddess Umā, wife of S'iva, when worshipped as a type of beauty and motherly excellence, is always regarded as a virgin. So in particular churches at Munich and Augsburg the shrines of the black Virgin are frequented by vast numbers of pilgrims, who hang up votive offerings, often consisting of waxen arms and legs, around her altar, in the firm belief that they owe the restoration of broken limbs and the recovery from various diseases to her intervention.

MONIER WILLIAMS.

We have reprinted the aforegoing by the kind permission of Professor Monier Williams, and have done so in the belief that the facts, therein recorded by that distinguished scholar for the first time, may illustrate a point of European folk-lore itself perhaps closely connected with a very obscure element of the ancient Italian mythology. We allude as well to the *Deae Matres* as also to the Fairies of Perrault. If we are to take the plain meaning of words only, the Mother Goddesses of India and the *Deae Matres* of Italy * should be the same deities, the races by whom the words were used being themselves identical. Professor Williams describes fully what are the attributes of the Indian deities. Of the attributes of the old Italian goddesses we know nothing beyond what is inferrible from their name. Neither S. Augustin, nor Arnobius, not even Marcianus Capella, all three generally full of curious information upon the minor powers of the Pantheon, make reference to them. We know that these goddesses were mothers. But of whom? presumably of the human race, for their rank is too low for any other maternity. If mothers of mankind they must be taken to have exhibited towards it the kindly feelings of maternity. They must have occasionally at least nurtured, protected, and benefitted their lowly children. Again, as the possession of power to do good involves the possession of a power usable at discretion, it may be inferred that the *Deae Matres* occasionally took offence and did harm. A race of supernatural beings so constituted still exists subjectively in the land of the old goddesses of Italy. In Sicily, where no doubt is entertained of their reality, they are called "outside women," "fair ladies," or "ladies" simply. So soon as a child is born it comes under the care and authority of one or more of these beings, who thenceforward become "padrone di casa," or mistresses of the house, and the human mother is subordinated to their higher maternity. When such human mother takes her child from its cradle she must ask leave of its invisible protectresses,—"by your leave my ladies" (cu licenza, signuri mei), she says in her soft dialect. An offence taken by them may bring down evil upon the mother or the child or both at the hands of the offended power. Signor Pitrè, the distinguished author of so much that is invaluable upon the subject of Sicily, her songs, her folk-tales, and her

---

* They are called "Matres Italae" in an inscription now in the British Museum. For a learned and exhaustive dissertation upon the "Matres," as well as the "Matronae," see a paper by W. M. Wylie, Esq. F.S.A. in the Archaeologia, vol. xlvi.

folk-lore, in a recent letter to me, sums up the case of these beings in the following most interesting words which I give as they are written.

"Le Donne di fuora, o Donne di loco, o Belle Signore o Signore, come si dicono con vari nomi, sono esseri sopranaturali che hanno della fata, e della strega, dotate di grande virtù, che esse possono trasmettere altrui. Esse amano od odiano, proteggono o perseguitano, beneficano o danneggiano a loro piacere o capriccio, a loro simpatia o antipatia. Sono abitatrici indefinite di case, o dell' aria, o del mondo sotterraneo, o de' boschi, amanti di congressi notturni, trasformantisi qualche volta in uccellacci, in gatti neri, in serpi. Proteggono cui vogliono far conquistare un tesoro, e gli fan vincere ostacoli d'ogni genere; danno la mala ventura a qualche povera ragazza; fanno aggobbare qualche creaturina che si trovi nella culla ovvero la fan trovare per terra; invisibili genii del male; o la cangiano con altra piu bella, o piu brutta, d'altro casato o d'altra prosapia. È col loro aiuto che puo togliersi d'addosso ad uno una malattia insanabile."

Signor Pitrè has already touched upon this curious theme in his recently published smaller work, "Usi natalizi nuziali e funebri del popolo Siciliano," to which we refer the reader (pp. 24, 43, 53). In the 13th volume of his "Biblioteca delle tradizioni popolari Siciliane" (Usi, Credenze, Superstizioni e Giuochi fanciulleschi), now shortly to appear, the subject will be found treated with the fulness and charm which are always to be recognised in the writings of this distinguished folk-lorist. In the "Donne di fuora" of Signor Pitrè we recognise the Fairies of Perrault, who attend the births and baptisms of princes and princesses, some favouring the child, others for offence taken exerting their supernatural powers to its detriment. In "La belle au bois dormant," all the fairies of the place are godmothers to the baby princess, and make her presents at her christening, "comme c'était la coutume des fées en ce temps là." The old fairy, however, who has been forgotten at the feast, revenges this neglect by the world-known lasting punishment, which she afterwards inflicts on the princess. In "Riquet à la houppe" a fairy repairs natural defects in two royal babies by a kind use of her supernatural powers.

HENRY CHARLES COOTE.

[In addition to the paper by Mr. W. M. Wylie in *Archaeologia*, mentioned by Mr. Coote, there is a paper by C. Roach Smith, F.S.A., and Thomas Wright, F.S.A., in *The Journal of the British Archæological Association* (vol. ii. pp. 239-255), which gives some additional information on the important subject of Mother-Worship. The paper is entitled " On certain Mythic Personages mentioned on Roman Altars found in England and on the Rhine." A fragment of Roman sculpture, discovered in the city of London, represents three females sitting, and holding in their laps baskets of fruit. This sculpture belongs to a class of female divinities, altars dedicated to whom have been found throughout England, the Netherlands, Belgium, along the banks of the Rhine, and in France and other countries. Among the inscriptions which Mr. Smith gives our own country has supplied analogies, such as—*matribus alatervis et matribus campestribus, deabus matribus, deabus matribus tramarinis, matribus domesticis, matribus,* and *matribus omnium gentium.* These are surely the local deities and the tribal or national deity of early Aryan mythology, as exemplified in Hindoo Mother-Worship. Their character is that of bestowing blessings; but in England an inscription has been found to them, as the three Lamiae, *Lamiis tribus,* which gives them also the character of evil and mischievous spirits, deceivers, witches. In connection with this paper another in the same volume should be referred to "On the Mythological Triad, as represented in the Eumenides of the Greeks," by T. R. Jones (pp. 315-323).—ED.]

NOTES, QUERIES, NOTICES, AND NEWS.

NOTES.

[*Communications for these columns should be addressed to the Hon. Secretary.*]

i. *Suffolk items.*—The following gleanings from East Suffolk (Beccles), the result of my Easter trip, may be of interest:—

Pigeon's feathers when stuffed into the pillow or mattress are thought to prolong the death-struggle. (This is a common superstition. Cf. *Henderson*, p. 60.)

The absence of rigor mortis is held to betoken fresh death in the family. I had this from the nurse of my cousin with whom I was staying. She believed in it devoutly. (Cf. *Folk-Lore Record*, vol. i. p. 51.)

It is unlucky to sit opposite the "jimmers" (*i. e.* the hinges) of the table when playing at cards.

The local name for the ladybird is "Bishy Barnaby." The superstitions are the usual ones.

Cold custard pudding is invariably eaten throughout East Suffolk on Easter Sunday.

ALFRED NUTT.

ii. *The Miller at the Professor's Examination* (ante, vol. ii. p. 173)—Reading over this story, I was struck with its likeness to two distinct stories current in the West of Scotland sixty years ago, one of them being printed as a chap-book within these fifty years, called *George Buchanan, the King's Fool;* the book was full of coarse wit that amused the youth. King James had laid a wager respecting the superiority in education of the Scotch over the English, and a high Professor was appointed as the referee. James, in order to gain the wager, applied to George, who undertook to outwit the Professor. George preceded the Professor dressed as a shepherd, and was seen tending a few sheep by the roadside and reading a book ; the Professor addressed him as to what he was reading, and found it a work in Latin, in which language they had converse for a time. George then hasted before the Professor and met him again in the garb of a ploughman. The Professor, putting a few questions about his education, was answered in Greek and Latin. For the third time George got a-head of the Professor, and was met in a still more humble guise, asking alms, which he did in Hebrew, Greek, and Latin, which so impressed the Professor that he turned back and gave the King the wager.

The Miller's story was told as having occured in Aberdeen. A learned Professor from Spain having visited Aberdeen University for some purpose put the question to the Senators if they had a professor of signs ? Although they did not know what this meant, still to keep up the character of the University they answered in the affirmative, thinking the Professor would not wait, and expressed their regret that he was out of town. But the Professor expressed his determination to see him before leaving, which put the Senators in great difficulty. Now, there lived in the town a sharp-witted shoemaker, who, when he had a glass, was ready for any project. The affair was stated to him, and he was willing to do anything for the honour of the city. The examination day came, and the shoemaker, in a Professor's dress, was introduced and seated opposite the Spanish Professor, with instruction he was not to speak but to sign his replies. So the Professor held up an orange, when the shoemaker at once held up a piece of oatcake ; the Professor then held up his forefinger, the shoemaker instantly held up two fingers ; the Professor now held up three fingers and thumb, which was followed by the shoemaker holding up his clenched fist in a menacing manner. The Professor then bowed his satisfaction, and the shoemaker withdrew. When the Professor said that he had never met such an educated man, such a man in his country would soon realise a fortune, seeing how easy they could communicate without language,—the other professors of Aberdeen were anxious to hear an explanation of the signs, which were afterwards explained thus : I held up an orange to say that my country produces such fruit ; he held up a cake in reply that your country produced the staff of life. I held up one finger to say I believe in one God ; he held up two, to say Father and Son. I then held up three and the thumb, to say Father, Son, and Holy Ghost are yet only one; he held up his entire hand, carrying out the full meaning of our creed, saying the same in substance, wisdom, and power. The professor then retired. The Senators were now anxious to hear the shoemaker's version of the signs, who being brought in to explain, said with triumphant glee, "You'll be nae mair fash wi' that character. He held up an orange, saying can you match that. I held a piece of cake, as much as to say that's worth all your oranges. He looked me in the face and pointing with his finger, as much as to say ye have but a'e e'e. I held up two to tell him my ane was worth his twa. He then held up three fingers and thumb, meaning that our three would only mak ane good one. This was too much, so I shook my neeve in his face, and he was glad to stop the quarrel that would have taken place." It will thus be seen that the two Scotch stories are from the same source, and probably other localities may have other versions. The George Buchanan story, as printed in Glasgow fifty years ago, is evidently of modern origin. Whether there be any connection between this way of explaining the learning exhibited by our labouring classes and the story of the professor of signs by either miller or shoemaker, is doubtful ; but as to the signs I think we must look far back for their origin. These signs are probably connected with ancient forms of blessing the people practised by the high priests in former ages, and I believe still practised by the Pope, when the three fingers are held up for the Trinity, &c. &c.

JAMES NAPIER.

iii. *Folk-Lore from British Guiana.*—" We passed a very large isolated rock of diorite, upon which were lying the bruised remains of a small tree branch, with many more around its base. These were the offerings left by Indian travellers at the shrine of the spirit of this rock, who believe that, if they did not perform the rite of breaking off a green bough and beating it on the rock, evil would most assuredly befall them."—*Canoe and Camp Life in British Guiana.* By C. Barrington Brown. Lond. 1876, p. 78.

" The first night after leaving Peaimah [on the Mazaruni] we heard a long, loud, and most melancholy whistle, proceeding from the direction of the depths of the forest, at which some of the men exclaimed, in an awed tone of voice, ' the Didi !' Two or three times the whistle was repeated, sounding like that made by a human being, beginning in a high key, and dying slowly and gradually away in a low one. There were conflicting opinions amongst the men regarding the origin of these sounds. Some said they proceeded from the wild hairy man, or ' Didi,' of the Indians ; others that they were produced by a large and poisonous snake. . . . . The ' Didi ' is said by the Indians to be a short, thick-set, and powerful wild man, whose body is covered with hair, and who lives in the forest. A belief in the existence of this fabulous creature is universal over the whole of British, Venezuelan, and Brazilian Guiana."—*Ibid.* pp. 87-8.

" We stopped in the forenoon to rest and feed, when we were startled by a most singular, prolonged cry, which made my Indians spring to their feet, listen intently, and then talk earnestly with bated breath. As there was something so human in the sound, I wished to go and see what it was, but the Indians would not stir a foot to accompany me, and fearing I should lose myself I gave up the idea. The Indians, ever ready with an improbable explanation, said that the sound must have proceeded from some Arecuna, who, having killed one of his own people, had been turned into a wild animal."—*Ibid.* p. 123.

" In the early morning, about 4 a.m. the Indians in these mountains, as well as those on the small savannas, become wakeful, and talk a good deal, some of them singing a most tuneless, dirge-like song. At Enamouta they added the noise of a drum to the performance, and at daylight they all issued from their houses simultaneously, greeting the morn with cries and loud shouts."—*Ibid.* p. 129.

" When on the point of leaving, a woman stepped forward to an old Indian in one of our canoes and held up her head. He tapped her forehead with his fingers, muttered a few words, and then blew towards her temple. This was done to charm away a pain in the head, the old fellow being a peaiman, and capable of effecting such cures.

On our arrival at villages I have sometimes seen a woman carry her infant round to one after another of the Indians of my party, each man as she passed stooping down and blowing gently on the face of the child."—*Ibid.* pp. 202-3.

Mr. Brown's guide on one occasion was a famed sorcerer, or peaiman, and at a village where they stopped one night he exercised his art for the benefit of a fever-stricken Indian. The peaiman left the house, saying that he had to go up amongst the mountains to roam about for the night, whilst his good spirit remained to cure the sick man, whose house he entered silently, and in the dark, after all the fires had been carefully put out. He presently commenced to chant, howl, and produce other discordant sounds, shaking at the same time a "shak-shak," or small calabash, filled with seeds, and fitted with a handle like a child's rattle, and beating with a palm-branch on the floor. Then he asked, in a deep, sepulchral voice, what ailed the patient, and the sick man's wife answered that some evil spirits or kanaimaks had "done him bad." The sorcerer said he would do his best, and called to his aid the good spirit of a bird (the maroodie), whose descent was imitated by the shaking of the palm-branch. The spirit complained of the long journey it had been suddenly required to make, but promised to do its best, and the discordant sounds, mingled with imitations of the maroudie's call, were resumed. The palm-leaf then fluttered towards the roof, and indicated the bird's departure, and after a dead silence made known the arrival of the spirit of an alligator, and afterwards of a duraquara, and so on. In some instances the wife asked the evil spirit how it could come and injure one who had never harmed it, begging it to desist and leave her husband alone. Her answer to this appeal was a most diabolical, mocking laugh. A little before daylight the sorcerer's body returned from the mountain and his spirit from ministering to the sick man.—*Ibid.* chap. vi. pp. 139-41.

At the foot of a mountain (Waetipu) were a row of small white quartz rocks, placed close together, and occupying a length of some fifty yards. The guide said that ages ago a party of Caribs came from the west and killed a gigantic tiger, and commemorated the event by depositing these stones, and by painting some red figures, which Mr. Brown unfortunately does not describe, in the cave where the monster had resided. The band afterwards destroyed a dangerous eagle, and returning towards the setting sun, were never seen again.—*Ibid.* chap. viii. p. 189.

When it was suggested that they should wash some rice which had been given to them, by dipping the earthern pot in the water, they demurred, saying " that if they placed their pot in the water the rain would fall more heavily."—*Ibid.* p. 397.

The same Indians begged the men " not to roast salt fish on the embers, fearing thereby to arouse the ire of a large eagle and Camoodie snake, which they said lived on the mountain side, and would show their displeasure by causing more rain to fall."—*Ibid.* p. 399.

The toes of a tapir " the men took off and saved for the purpose of using, when occasion required, as charms for bites of snakes, stings of rayfish, and fits of all kinds. They said that the hoofs are first singed, and then placed in water, which is drunk as a remedy." Perhaps the ammonia, adds Mr. Brown, may have some good effect.—*Ibid.* p. 240.

Near the village of Apoterie were " some large granite rocks, in passing which our Carib turned away his face in an opposite direction. Upon questioning him as to his reason for so doing, I learned that if he looked at them he would get fever."—*Ibid.* p. 244.

" It is a popular belief in the tropics that sleeping in the moonlight twists one's mouth, and I used to go to sleep haunted by the reflection that perhaps on waking next morning I should find my mouth inconveniently turned towards one ear."—*Ibid.* p. 278.

An old Indian woman told them that all the people of the village had been to visit the sorcerer of Wakopyeng, who, " among other wonderful performances, could make himself invisible at times, and had a little bottle full of fire."—*Ibid.* p. 285-286.

" In most Indian houses pieces of thick, roughly-plated fibre or cord, as thick as cod-line, and a yard in length, are seen hanging up in the roof. These have all been passed up through the nose of the owner of the house, and drawn out by the mouth, for the purpose of giving him good luck in hunting."—*Ibid.* p. 302-303.

" On our way we passed a deep pool, where there was an eddy, in which the guide informed us there lived a 'water child' covered with long hair. A woodskin with Indians was passing the spot one day, when the water child came to the surface, caught hold of and upset the canoe. One of its occupants sank with it, and, being seized by the child, never came to the surface again."—*Ibid.* p. 392.

THOMAS SATCHELL.

iv. *Marriage custom.*—The curious old custom of showering grain over a couple newly married, being the expression by sign of a wish that fecundity might crown the union, is a common accompaniment of weddings in Bristol. Rice is used for convenience, but wheat was of old the chosen grain. When Henry VII. brought his bride to Bristol on the sen'night following Whitsunday, 1486, " a baker's wife cast out of a window a great quantity of wheat, crying Welcome! and Good Luck! "— Seyer's *Memorials*, cap. xxii. par. 6. This morning, April 10th, 1880, girls and women were rushing into grocers' shops in the locality of the Broad Quay to buy each a quarter of a pound of rice, with which to salute a quay lumper and his bride as they came out of church. Yesterday the newspaper recounting certain ceremonies connected with a fashionable wedding at Clifton states that rice was freely thrown over the bridal party as they left the church. The practice is without doubt a survival of Roman occupation. And it is commonly practised elsewhere.

J. F. NICHOLLS, F.S.A.

v. *Bristol local custom.*—There is also another curious local custom, confined, I believe, to one street only in this city. When an inhabitant of Back Street dies the whole surface of the street from end to end is covered with sand. Back Street was the site of King John's House, outside the walls of the borough, and since that date it may reasonably be supposed to have been a favoured residence of the Welsh, as

it runs parallel to the quay known as the Welsh Back. Is the above
a Welsh custom ? or is anything of the kind practised in Italy ?

J. F. NICHOLLS, F.S.A. (Bristol).

vi. *Witchcraft and other superstitions.*—The following is from the
Morning Advertiser for September 13, 1822 :—

" *Witchcraft.*—The following curious letter is copied from a manuscript in the British Museum :—

" *From Mr. Manning, Dissenting Teacher, at Halstead, in Essex, to
John Morley, Esq. Halstead.*

" Halstead, Aug. 2, 1732.

" SIR,—The narrative which I gave you in relation to witchcraft,
and which you are pleased to lay your commands upon me to repeat,
is as follows:—There was one master Collett, a smith by trade, of
Haveningham, in the county of Suffolk, who, as 'twas customary
with him, assisting the maide to churn, and not being able (as the
phrase is) to make the butter come, threw a hot iron into the churn,
under the notion of witchcraft in the case, upon which a poore labourer,
then employed in carrying dung in the yard, cried out in a terrible
manner, ' They have killed me, they have killed me,' still keeping his
hand upon his back, intimating where the pain was, and died upon the
spot. Mr. Collett, with the rest of the servants then present, took off
the poor man's cloathes, and found, to their great surprise, the mark
of the iron that was heated and thrown into the churn deeply impressed
upon his back. This account I had from Mr. Collett's own mouth,
who, being a man of an unblemished character, I very [*sic*] believe to
be matter of fact.—I am, Sir, your obliged humble servant,

" *Sam Manning.*"

In the same paper for Sept. 21 following is a letter referring to
this, signed A. C. R., from which the following are extracts :—"There
is a curious practice not yet exploded on the Continent, and still in
full vigour among the farmers in France. It is held as a great mystery,
and I was entrusted with the knowledge of it several years ago, when
I was there. When a woman is in the act of churning, if any one

repeats backwards, letter by letter, the following words from Psalm lxxxvi. 6—*Memor ero Rahab, et Babilonis scientium me*—she may churn, churn, and churn away till she is utterly tired, no sort of coagulation will take place. But if some more powerful conjuror, with churner herself, pronounces the inverted word *Irarobal—Laborari*, I have worked—from another Psalm, the milk soon thickens, and the butter appears."

If the operation of caponising, which is performed by women, be witnessed by a man, the fowl will die. This is given as existing " at this moment " in Normandy, and other provinces of France near Paris.

" Shepherds are supposed to be the most experienced wizards; you meet them in a lonely vale at dusk ; they ask you the hour of the day ; if you do not answer with becoming politeness they make you roam about all night without your ever being able to find your way home, till the dawn of morn dispel their charms."

" A bum-bailiff went to a village to perform his duty. Passing through an orchard, and being very thirsty, he plucks three blooming, red-velveted peaches from a tree, and eats them. On his returning home he is taken with such excruciating pains in his bowels that he doubts not but the fruit has been bewitched. He calls for a wizard, by whose order three leaves from the enchanted tree are brought to the bum-bailiff; he places them under his pillow, and for the first time, after two days of the greatest misery, he falls into the arms of sleep, but is soon awakened by a hard knocking at his door. ' Oh, for God's sake, Sir, let me say a few words to you ; I am tortured, I am dying.' The poor devil is admitted, and, confessing that a much more clever sorcerer had put him in this terrible plight, desires the pain-working leaves to be removed from under the pillow. His prayer is complied with; he feels instantly relieved; and walks home free from his bellyache and his fears."

JAMES BRITTEN.

vii. *Death Superstition.*—I copied the following from a MS. diary of a deceased relative in West Sussex :—

Extract from " A Fortnight's Tour to Brighton, Lewes, Ditchling,
and adjacent Villages (from Arundel), August, 1820."

Friday 11th, Sompting.

" Whilst the woman was dying I was standing at the foot of the
bed, when a woman desired me to remove, saying, ' You should never
stand at the foot of a bed when a person is dying.'   The reason, I
ascertained, was because it would stop the spirit in its departure to
the unknown world.

" Immediately after the woman was dead, I was requested by the
persons in attendance to go with them into the garden to awake the
bees, saying it was a thing which ought always to be done when a
person died after sunset. [See ante, vol. i. p. 59 (192) ; Henderson's
Folk Lore of Northern Counties, pp. 309-10.]

" I reasoned with them on the absurdity of the practice, but it was
in vain, for they actually went out at midnight and did awake them."

ALPHEUS SMITH.

viii. *Curious Good Friday Observances.*—At the Church of All
Hallows, Lombard Street, according to a custom which has been observed for the last 287 years, sixty of the younger boys from Christ's
Hospital attended the service, after which, in accordance with the will
of Peter Symonds, made in 1593, they each received at the hands of
the churchwarden, Mr. Shayer, a new penny and a packet of raisins.
The same will also directs that the clerk and sexton shall receive 6*d.*
each, the Rector of Chadwell, in Essex, 20*s.*, and the poor of the
parish and ward and the Sunday-school children 6*d.* each.

A very ancient custom was again observed at St. Bartholomew-the-
Great, Smithfield.   At the conclusion of the service an old tomb in
the churchyard was visited (a procession being formed), when the Rev.
J. Morgan laid twenty-one sixpences on the tomb, which were picked
up by twenty-one elderly females of the parish.   It is stated that an
old lady left this benefaction, and that she lies buried in the churchyard, but the exact spot cannot be pointed out.   The scene yesterday
was of a disorderly character, owing to a number of boys and girls

having taken possession of the place, thus preventing many of the respectable inhabitants attending the ancient ceremony.—*Daily Telegraph*, 27 March, 1880.

ix. *Russian Superstition.*—The hangman is permitted to trade upon the superstition still current in Russian society respecting the luck conferred upon gamesters by the possession of a morsel of the rope with which a human being has been strangled, either by the hand of justice or by his own. Immediately after young Mladctzky had been hanged, only the other day, Froloff was surrounded by members of the Russian jeunesse dorée, eager to purchase scraps of the fatal noose ; and he disposed of several dozen such talismans at from three to five roubles apiece, observing, with cynical complacencey, when he had sold off his last remnant, that " he hoped the Nihilists would yet bring him in plenty of money."—*Daily Telegraph*, 27 March, 1880.

x. *Wendish Superstition.*—A strange and horrible Wendish superstition, which has been handed down from the Pagan ancestors of the Prussians proper of to-day to their descendants peopling the German shores of the Baltic and the Brandenburg Marches, has of late led with shocking frequency to the commission of a hideous crime, punishable, even under the merciful German laws, by life-long imprisonment. It is commonly believed among the poorer peasantry of Wendish extraction that several paramount medicinal virtues and magical charms are seated in the heart or liver of a dead maiden or infant of tender years, and that these organs, brewed with certain herbs into a beverage, will cure diseases or inspire the passion of love in their consumers. The practical result of this barbarous belief is the constantly recurrent violation of the grave's sanctity, and the mutilation of the corpses secretly disinterred from the consecrated ground in which they have been laid to rest. Last week two graves in the new cemetery of Weissensee were broken open during the night, the coffins contained in them forced, and the bodies of an unmarried girl and a male infant discovered next morning by the guardians of the burial-ground, mangled in the most revolting manner, the cavity of the chest in both cases

having been completely emptied of its contents. A rigid search for
the perpetrators of this ghastly offence is being instituted by the gen-
darmerie of the Weissensee district, but with small hope of success, as
the superstitious savages, who have upon several occasions within the
last few years committed several similar outrages, have hitherto invariably escaped detection.—*Daily Telegraph*, 26 May, 1880.

QUERIES.

[*Communications for these columns should be addressed to the Hon. Secretary.*]

i. *Irish Traditions.*—In the *Gentleman's Magazine* for May 1832,
p. 406, is printed " A relation of a rat which followed and ever would
be with that worthy gentleman, Sir Edward Norris, then residing in
Ireland."

" Some curious traditionary stories connected with this tale," says the
writer, " are still related to the visitors of Mallow Castle, in Ireland,
now the seat of C. D. O. Jephson, Esq. M.P." Are these traditionary
stories still told, and where can an account of them be obtained ?

G. L. GOMME.

ii. Beda says of Ethelbert of Kent that he would not allow Augus
tine and his companions to come to him in any house, lest, " according
to an ancient superstition," if they practised any magical arts, they
might impose upon him and so get the better of him. (*Ecc. Hist.*
bk. i. cap. 25.) Is there in modern Folk-Lore any survival of this
ancient superstition ?

G. L. GOMME.

iii. *Florentine Folk-Lore.*—Can any of your correspondents tell me
why on Ascension Day at Florence they sell beetles, crickets in cages,
walk about with them, and give them to their loved ones ?

S. B.

NOTICES AND NEWS.

i. *Sixty Folk-Tales from Montale.* Collected by Gherardo Nerucci (Sessanta novelle popolari Montalesi, circondario di pistoia, raccolte da Gherardo Nerucci. Fireuze. Successori Le Monnier.) 1880. [1 vol. pp. vi. 506.]

This is a further contribution to the fast increasing stock of Italian Folk-Tales.

Of Signor Nerucci's stories many have already appeared, namely, in the Collections of Professors Comparetti and Imbriani, and also in a public journal of Italy.

In the autumn of 1868 Signor Nerucci, who is a distinguished philologist, commenced his task of collecting from the peasants of his own district of Montale the popular stories still current there, and his perseverance and acumen have been amply rewarded by the interesting results now before us.

No one could be better adapted for this self-imposed labour than Signor Nerucci. So familiar is he with the dialect of Montale, and the modes of thought and expression of its people, that he feels competent to take upon himself the rehearsal of those tales, before a sympathetic but critical rustic audince, in their own Montalese vernacular. He knows the tales as well as their best story-tellers. He knows them, also, not only as one person tells them, but as all who are acquainted with them tell them. One tells them in one way, and one in another, one shortens them, one lengthens them, all, however, adhering closely to settled *motifs* from which they never depart.

Of the stories thus published by Signor Nerucci, a great part are told, with unimportant variations, in other parts of Italy. Some, however, are not so paralleled, and, if not original inventions of Italy, are sole survivors out of a stock now lost. In either case, however, the

tales are equally valuable, for reasons which will readily suggest themselves.

Nowhere except in Italy could such sallies of bright thought and
happy language be unearthed in a district no bigger than an English
hundred.   So small a periphery would no where else inclose so much
that is taking in feeling, dialogue, and description.   Through them
all gleams the natural fine taste that knows how to reconcile the
grotesque wonders of fairyland with good sense, steering clear of mere
absurdity and *bétise*—a fault so visible in the Russian tales.

In addition to this quality, prominently shown in the present collection is the freedom of language which distinguishes the Tuscan, the
tales being told in a sub-dialect of Etruria, which, like its parent, bears
close resemblance to Aulic or Italian.

It would be no slight task to lay before the reader the details of
these sixty stories, or even of those which we consider as qualifiedly
original, and it is not our intention to do so.   We will only call
attention to the two charmingly told tales of *Zuccaccia* and *Bellindia*,
which have already appeared in our pages, and to these we will add,
as particularly deserving of notice where all are good, the gloriously
quaint tale of " Testa di bufala."

We advise our readers who are acquainted with the Italian language
to possess themselves of this volume, for in its possession they will
have intellectual enjoyment of many kinds.

A particularly interesting (not to say important) class of stories,
prominent in this volume, are what we may call " Arabian Nights "
stories.   The English reader may not be aware that fictions, undoubtedly
referrible to this stock, exist everywhere in Italy.

Signor Nerucci gives us charming versions of the Forty Thieves—
the Peri Banou, the Jealous Sisters, and one of the Calender's tales.
They are respectively called " Cicerchia o i ventidue ladri." " I tre regali
o la novella de tappeti." " Il figliolo del re di Francia," and " Il canto
e l' sono della Sara Sibilla."

They are all, however, thoroughly Italianised, and betray nothing
of their oriental origin.   Upon this arises a most curious problem.
Are these stories mere adaptations of M. Galland's " Mille et une

nuits," or are they importations from the East made at an earlier but unknown period ? Of these, however, the Jealous Sisters certainly need not have been taken from Galland, because it is given by Straparola in his "Notti Piarevoli" long before Galland existed; and perhaps this circumstance may raise a presumption in favour of the earlier advent of the others. Upon this point the learned will have to decide some day, and, when they consider the subject, they will at the same time have to grapple with a further difficulty, viz., neither the Forty Thieves, Peri Banou, nor the Jealous Sisters has ever been found in an eastern manuscript, nor heard by any European from the lips of an eastern storyteller. Whence, then, did M. Galland get them ?

We should add that Signor Nerucci informs us in his preface, that at the present time there prevails in the Peninsula a feverish activity for collecting folk-tales. We are glad to hear it. Though so much has been done by Italians for Italy and Sicily, there still remain certain districts not yet worked, but which it is very desirable should be gleaned. We will add Rome and her territory to this list—not out of disrespect to Mrs. Busk, whose admirable work we appreciate at its own high value—but we hold that such an important centre should be entirely exhausted by native collectors, and that the tales should be produced in their vernacular form.

ii. *Contribuiçoes para uma Mythologia Popular Portugueza.* 1. As superstiçõos populares na legislação religiosa. 2. As bruxas na tradicção de nosso povo. Por Z. Consiglieri Pedroso, Professor de Historia no Curso Superior de Lettras de Lisboa. Porto. Imprensa Commercial. Rua dos Lavadouros, 16. 1880.

iii. *Ensaios Criticos.* 1. A Mythologia das Plantas de A. de Gubernatis. 2. A Mythologia Comparada de Girard de Rialle. Por Z. Consiglieri Pedroso, Professor de Historia no Curso Superior de Lettras, Porto. Imprensa Commercial. Rua dos Lavadouros, 16. 1879.

[Contributions for a Popular Mythology of Portugal—the Popular

Superstitions in Religious Legislation : the Witches in the Tradition of our People.

Critical Essays—The Mythology of Plants of A. de Gubernatis : The Comparative Mythology of Girard de Rialle.] (*Pamphlets.*)

We have been favoured with these interesting works by the learned Professor himself.

In the first of them Professor Pedroso remarks—"For the study of the superstitions of our people, and, under a more general point of view, for the constitution of a popular Portuguese mythology, we have two sources to explore. The first is oral tradition. The second are documents principally of the sixteenth, seventeenth, and eighteenth centuries. Of these sources the first is beyond dispute the most important. In the second category are included proceedings of the Inquisition, legislative enactments, and writings of authors."

As regards documentary evidence, the proceedings of the Inquisition afford the largest contingent, but they are still only imperfectly known. More than 80,000 of these processes are in actual existence. Of positive legislation there is one document as early as A.D. 1385. There are numerous religious constitutions on this subject, *e.g.* one of the Archbishop of Evora, in 1534, and this latter is the richest list of popular superstitions we have ever met with, its perusal demonstrating also that Portugal is or was, on such matters, entirely at one with all the Latin nations in general, ourselves included. The bit of rope by which a criminal has been suspended brings luck and averts disaster as surely in Portugal as we know it always has done in England [and in Russia; see *ante*, page 137]. It is easy, therefore, to see that Portugal is rich in evidence of popular superstitions. It should be observed that the twofold method recommended by Professor Pedroso is one which has been already followed by Signor Pitrè in regard to Sicily, and no doubt can exist of its efficacy and appropriateness.

This is a most interesting paper, and should, we think, be translated in its entirety for production in our journal.

The next paper—on witches—is still more interesting, as being fuller of facts and details. This also, we think, should be reproduced to our readers in our own vernacular. The nature and *indoles* of the Portuguese witch are critically examined and determined by Professor Pedroso. " She has no affinity to the fays (fadas). The latter are a true Providence for the unfortunate and innocent. They discover treasures, give riches, deliver from dangers, marry orphans and found-lings to millionaire princes, &c." The witch is an entirely different being, always and wholly maleficent. She is not self-constituted, but is admitted to her degree. In the " confession of certain witches, who were burnt in the city of Lisbon, A.D. 1559, MS. Sentences of the Inquisition, vol. i.," it is said " no one can be a witch (*bruja*) without going through the degrees of *feiticeyra* and *alcoviteyra*." The *feiticeyra* is an old woman who has made a lesser pact with the devil for certain advantages to be conferred upon her. The *bruja*, in popular tradition, is more highly endowed. She is constituted also much more formally. She is sworn upon a black book without a single white leaf in it. Two devils stand on each side of her, while a third holds the book. The form of oath is known, for it has been proved in a court of law. When witches are minded to join the Devil's *conciliabulum*, at a cross road, they anoint themselves with some special unguent, and, on the repetition of a fit formula of words, they instantaneously join a motley throng of Portuguese, Moors, Jews, Frenchmen, and others. They have a good time of it till cock-crow or the name of Jesus disperses them. All this is Latin and English tradition also.

Though witches generally require to be made, yet some may be said to be born. If a woman has seven daughters, without an intervening son, the seventh becomes a witch. There is an antidote for this, however, if her parents will only take care to have her baptized Mary, or some other name of the Holy Family. Analo-gously to this a seventh son, under like circumstances, becomes a were-wolf (lobishomen).

There is much more in these interesting tracts of Professor Pedroso. But our space permits us only to intimate to the reader what a rich mine they contain upon the subject of what Professor Pedroso elegantly and justly designates " the anonymous creations of the popular genius " (as creaçoes anonymas do genio popular).

In conclusion we will mention that the Professor refers to an unedited collection of Folk Tales of Portugal which he has prepared. Can he not permit them to be published in the pages of the " Folk-Lore Record "?

The titles of the two critical essays which Professor Pedroso has also sent declare their contents. He has been lavish therein of his learning and judgment, and we recommend them to the attentive perusal of such of our readers as are acquainted with the Portugese language.

iv. *Elizabethan Demonology.* An essay in illustration of the belief in the existence of Devils, and the powers possessed by them, as it was generally held during the period of the Reformation and the times immediately succeeding ; with special reference to Shakspere and his works. By Thomas Alfred Spalding, LL.B. (Chatto and Windus 1880) [1 vol. pp. xii. 151.]

As Mr. Furnivall has said, this book is primarily a Shakspere book ; but it is so mainly because it seeks to interpret Shakspere's use of Folk-Lore by obtaining a knowledge of the Folk-Lore current in Queen Elizabeth's time. Thus Mr. Spalding's book is eminently useful to Folk-Lorists. It unearths and arranges much that was unknown of the popular superstitions of the time in the matter of devil-worship and belief in spirits, witches, &c.; and it rightly rejects the theory that Shakspere, an artist—and an artist, too, who knew and studied the English people, would, in the first place, apply to a foreign source for his materials for the weird sisters of *Macbeth* when he had got English materials already to hand, and then, after having thus obtained his needs from Norse mythology, would have maltreated them and made them neither English nor Norse. The weird sisters, as Mr. Spalding shows, represent to the full the beliefs of English country-people in Elizabeth's time, and by studying their characteristics and tracing out their origin some good work is done for Shakspere lovers—and who is not so ?—and for Folk-Lorists. It is well not to overlook the importance of chronological accounts of the prevalence of popular superstitions, because by these we can test the permanence of the survival of primitive culture, and we can note the changes that have arisen from epoch to epoch, and so possibly gain an insight into the laws of the change.

v. *Folk-Lore Journal.* Edited by the Working Committee of the South African Fork-Lore Society. Vol. i. parts 5 and 6. Vol. ii. part 1. September, 1879, to January, 1880. (Cape Town : Darter Brothers and Walton. London : David Nutt).

It is much to be regretted that this Journal has not been more extensively supported in England. Folk-Lorists are much indebted to it. In the present numbers, besides native Folk-Tales, all of value, papers are given on Letshuâna proverbs, five Herero sayings or proverbs, the annual festivals of the Zulus, and some minor superstitions and customs of the Zulus connected with children.

vi. *Indian Fairy Tales,* collected and translated by Maive Stokes. With Notes by Mary Stokes, and an Introduction by W. R. S. Ralston, M.A. Ellis and White. 1880. [1 vol. pp. xxxii. 304.]

Folk-tales from India are always welcome. They are usually interesting, and they are often valuable, filling up gaps in the collections for which we are indebted to oriental literature, and offering suggestive contrasts and parallels to the similar stories of Europe. But they are usually scattered over the pages of periodicals, or embedded in costly books of travel. All who seriously study Folk-Lore will therefore be grateful to Miss Maive Stokes, the very young daughter of the well-known Celtic scholar, Mr. Whitley Stokes, for the admirable collection and translation she has made of thirty "Indian Fairy Tales," told to her by two Hindu ayahs and a Muhammadan man-servant. Her work forms an excellent companion to Miss Bartle Frere's charming book of a similar kind, "Old Deccan Days"; which, however, differs from it slightly, inasmuch as Miss Frere's ayah was a native Christian.

The · Notes, occupying 57 pages, with which .the late Mrs. Whitley Stokes has enriched it, are thoroughly good, testifying to a remarkably wide range of reading, a cultivated intelligence, and sound judgment.   The stories themselves may be roughly classified as follows :— Among the most important are those which illustrate some of the well-known themes or characters of European popular fiction.   Such are No. 10, a "husk myth" of the "Beauty and the Beast" class, in which a princess marries a monkey, and turns him by her love from a beast into a fairy prince.   No. 20 is a good specimen of the "Goldenlocks" tale, describing the final triumph of a brilliant being temporarily obscured.   The "Fan Prince," No. 25, belongs to the familiar "Blue Bird" cycle.   To the large class of tales in which children are persecuted by a stepmother, and are killed, but brought to life again, belongs No. 2, the "Pomegranate King."   No. 1, "The Pink-rose Queen," and No. 14, "Loving Laili," are valuable contributions to the stock of mysterious tales about heroines who are cruelly persecuted, often being deprived of even their good looks, but who, after strange transformations, emerge from their troubles in triumph.   Such ladies are often driven away for a time from their lords by "Substituted Brides."   To the number of princesses thus afflicted belong the heroines of No. 21, "The Bel-Princess," and No. 23, "The Princess who loved her father like salt."   No. 27 is the tale of the faithful servant whom his lord's wife tries to kill.   No. 26 describes how the troubles of a youth were brought to a close by the valuable information given to him by the four legs of his bed, which successively went out " to eat the air." The large class of stories describing the feats of a hero who is constantly warring with demons, and frequently marrying their daughters, is well represented by Nos. 11 and 24, in each of which figures a mysterious being like " The Giant who had no heart in his body" of the Norse Tales, the "Punchkin" of " Old Deccan Days," and by No. 22, "How the Raja's Son won the Princess Labam."   No. 6, "The Voracious Frog," is a good specimen of the tales about a devouring monster, which swallows all it meets, until at last it is obliged to disgorge its victims, who emerge unhurt.   A very good specimen also of the stories about destiny is No. 12, relating the travels of " The Man who went to seek his Fate." No. 8, " Barber Him and the Tigers," is one of the facetious narratives in which the Great are discomfited by the Small. To the class of comic tales belong, also, No. 7, " The Story of Foolish Sachuli," and the " Lie-stories," in Nos. 4, 17, and 18, as well as No. 3, which explains that " all cats are aunts to the tigers." As " moral tales " may be considered Nos. 5, 9, and 30, as well as several stories derived from Indian literature, and closely associated with Indian beliefs. Such are Nos. 13 and 29, which sing the praises of the meek monarch Harichandra; No. 15, which tells " How King Burtal became a Fakir ;" No. 16, devoted to " Some of the doings of Shekh Farid ;" and No. 19, a tale illustrating Indian ideas about divine justice and a future life. The Clever Wife of No. 28, also, belongs to literature, and has passed from that of the East into that of the West. The stories are preceded by an introduction, 23 pages long, by Mr. W. R. S. Ralston, calling attention to the close connexion between the Folk-Tales of India and Europe. One of the special charms of the tales, it should be remarked, is their style—simple, clear, often quaint, the words in which they are told, those of a very young girl, are exactly such as best befit the class of popular fictions to which they belong. The book is one which may be warmly recommended both to old and young,

At the last Evening Meeting of the Society the Rev. J. Long brought forward the importance of collecting and arranging the proverbs of England and their parallels in other lands. His paper is printed at pages 56—79 of the present volume. The Council feel that the subject is a most important one, and in order to carry out the suggestion of Mr. Long they propose that at the Annual Meeting of the Society in June a Committee be appointed of Members of the Society to consider and report to the Council the best means of collecting and arranging English proverbs, with a view to future publication. Any Members who will take part in the work of the Committee are requested to communicate at once to the Honorary Secretary.

The author of *Brazil, the Amazons, and the Coast* (by Herbert H. Smith, Sampson Low and Co.) gives some curious specimens of the Folk-Lore of the Amazonian Indians, and he intimates his intention of collecting and comparing other similar matter from a much wider tract.—*The Athenæum*, 22nd May, 1880. p. 659.

Members will be glad to hear that Messrs. Ellis and White have published the *Indian Fairy Tales* of Miss Maive Stokes (aged 13). The book contains, besides the stories taken down from the lips of native servants, a valuable introduction by Mr. W. R. S. Ralston.

Mr. J. T. Micklethwaite, F.S.A., is engaged upon a collection of *Church Folk-Lore*, and would be glad of any items sent to him.

Mr. Alfred Nutt has prepared a table in blank form, by which Folk-Tales can be classified according to Von Hahn's scheme, and another for comparison with Grimm's *Kinder und Hausmärchen*. Mr. Nutt intends printing similar forms for use in classifying under Baring-Gould's scheme and under his own scheme. These forms are arranged in columns, to be filled up by each collector or student, and Mr. Nutt promises to let any Member of the Society have a copy upon application to him at his residence, Rosendale Hall, West Dulwich, S.E.

Mr. Nutt would be glad to receive bibliographical notes on English Folk-Tales, and early references to them in English literature.

Subscriptions (One Guinea per annum) should be paid to the Union Bank of London (Charing Cross Branch) to the credit of the Society. To avoid inconvenience, and to insure punctual payment, it is requested that members will furnish their bankers or agents with authority (by signing and forwarding to them an order, to be obtained from the Honorary Secretary) to pay their annual subscription to the Society.

The publications of the Society are : —

For 1878 :—

The Folk-Lore Record, vol. i. [*Issued.*]

For 1879 :—

Notes on the Folk-Lore of the Northern Counties of England and the Borders. By William Henderson. A new edition, with considerable additions by the author. [*Issued*].

Aubrey's Remains of Gentilisme and Judaisme, with the additions by Dr. White Kennet. Edited by James Britten, F.L.S. [*In the press.*]

The Folk-Lore Record, vol. ii. together with the Annual Report for 1878. [*Issued.*]

For 1880 :—

The Denham Tracts. Edited by James Hardy.

The Folk-Lore Record, vol. iii. (in two half-yearly parts), together with the Annual Report for 1879. [*In the press.*]

For 1881 (selected from the following):—

Folk-Medicine. By William George Black.

Folk-Lore and Provincial Names of British Birds. By the Rev. C. Swainson.

Notes on the Folk-Lore of the North-East of Scotland. By the Reverend Walter Gregor. [*In the press.*]

In course of early preparation:—

Bibliography of English Works on Folk-Lore.

Excerpts from two Early-English Folk-Lorists.

Notes for a History of English Chapbooks and Penny Histories.

East Sussex Superstitions. By the Reverend W. D. Parish.

The Merry Tales of the Wise Men of Gotham. To be Edited, with illustrative Notes and an Introductory Essay on English Noodledom, by William J. Thoms, F.S.A.

Folk-Lore from the Gentleman's Magazine. By G. L. Gomme, F.S.A.

The Folk-Lore of Lincolnshire. By Edward Peacock, F.S.A.

Index to the Folk-Lore in "Notes and Queries." By James Britten, F.L.S.

On Madagascar Folk-Lore. By the Reverend J. Sibree.

On Chinese Folk-Lore. By Dr. N. B. Dennys.

The Officers of the Society
FOR 1880.

PRESIDENT.

THE RIGHT HON. THE EARL BEAUCHAMP, F.S.A.

VICE-PRESIDENTS.

HENRY CHARLES COOTE, ESQ., F.S.A.

W. R. S. RALSTON, ESQ., M.A.

EDWARD B. TYLOR, ESQ., LL.D., F.R.S.

COUNCIL.

EDWARD BRABROOK, F.S.A.

JAMES BRITTEN, F.L.S.

DR. ROBERT BROWN.

SIR W. R. DRAKE, F.S.A.

G. L. GOMME, F.S.A.

HENRY HILL, F.S.A.

A. LANG, M.A.

F. OUVRY, F.S.A.

PROFESSOR A. H. SAYCE.

EDWARD SOLLY, F.R.S. F.S.A.

WILLIAM J. THOMS, F.S.A.

W. S. W. VAUX, M.A.

DIRECTOR.—WILLIAM J. THOMS, F.S.A

TREASURER.—SIR WILLIAM R. DRAKE, F.S.A.

HONORARY SECRETARY.—G. L. GOMME, F.S.A., Castelnau, Barnes, S.W.

AUDITORS.—JOHN TOLHURST, ESQ.

J. S. UDAL, ESQ.

BANKERS.—UNION BANK OF LONDON, CHARING CROSS BRANCH, to whom all Subscriptions should be paid.